WIND BENEATH MY WINGS

Cowgirls in Time Romance Series

A Chill Wind

Wind Beneath My Wings

WIND BENEATH MY WINGS

Erica Einhorn

Ralston Store Publishing
P.O. Box 1684
Prescott, Arizona 86302

ISBN 978-1-938322-23-5

Professionally and lovingly edited by:
Jennifer Hope
www.MesaVerdeMediaServices.com

Printed in the USA.

Dedicated to the one I love

CHAPTER ONE

SARAH FOUND IT an interesting experience living between two different centuries. It was not taxing; there was no hardship involved—except the natural hardships defined by the times—like the lack of toilets and cell phones. It felt more like two separate cultures combined into one place. Actually, it was two distinct places—the old Red Bluff and the new Red Bluff. But it was all Red Bluff, all home to Sarah. Sometimes she even felt more at home while she visited the old Red Bluff. In many ways, she felt more comfortable there.

She had been feeling lonely. Her friend Jenna had moved to the old Red Bluff a while ago, and now Sarah could only see her on weekends. And Sarah's job at the attorney's office annoyed her. Since she had—how should she put it—fallen out of love with Marcus, the job was a lot less interesting.

Yes, she knew it was good that she had let go of the fantasy of herself and Marcus. Jenna didn't need to tell her that Marcus was happily married and not interested in having an affair or—what Sarah had hoped for all along—leaving his wife to marry Sarah. Fantasy, fantasy,

1

fantasy. Now that she felt over him, she hated that she had wasted so much of her life on a dead-end dream. How many years had it been? Too long to even want to remember how long.

So her job bored her, and she could only talk to her best friend Jenna on the weekend; what did she have left? Singing. Sarah loved her weekends staying at the hotel in the old Red Bluff and singing Friday and Saturday nights at the local saloon. She lived for that. It made her feel alive and appreciated.

The old Red Bluff. Sarah didn't know what else to call it. Jenna had accidentally discovered a cave that took them from their own time into the Red Bluff of 1870. Then Jenna had married the sheriff and moved there. And now Sarah lived for her weekends in the old Red Bluff.

Thankfully, she now prepared for another delightful, satisfying weekend. Her weekends there made her feel fulfilled because although she just worked for tips, people tipping her with their own hard-earned money made her feel good. It was normally only a few dollars a night, but it paid for her hotel. Lately, the tips had gone up. She supposed that people were beginning to appreciate her more. Often, she received a gold coin. When she sold it at the coin store in her own time, it usually made her more money than a week on her regular dreary job. Lately, she noticed that she was getting at least one gold coin a night.

As she stuffed the second dress into the small soft-sided suitcase that she would attach to the back of her saddle, she thought maybe she would ask Jenna if she could leave some clothes at her house in the old Red Bluff. That would make packing easier. No, that wouldn't work, either. Sarah didn't like to wear the same dress twice in one year.

Clothes. They made her feel good. She liked strutting her stuff around in a pretty dress. And she didn't care that she was the only one at the office who wore a different dress every day. Sarah would not allow herself to feel guilty over her clothes. She made good money working for the attorneys, and she could spend it any way she pleased. Wearing new clothes all the time made her feel good, made her feel more feminine. It made her smile.

Sarah zipped up the suitcase, stuck it in her car, and drove over to Jenna's ranch. Correction. Jenna's old ranch. Now, since Jenna moved to the old Red Bluff, Jenna's niece, Madison, lived on the ranch. She took good care of the house and property, took good care of the horses and cows, but it wasn't the same. Sarah used to enjoy coming here. Now, it was just the place to pick up her horse, Dancer.

Dancer nickered when he saw her. Sarah walked over to him and handed him an apple. "Good boy. Do you love *me* or the apples that I bring you?" she asked. Dancer greedily ate the apple and then nuzzled Sarah. "Okay, you *do* love me! That makes me feel better, Dancer!" She stroked his neck.

She slowly brushed him, noting that his winter coat had almost disappeared. His coat was getting back to its summer sleekness. She saddled him, bridled him, and attached her soft-sided suitcase to the back of the saddle. Walking him through the gate to the paddock, she wondered if she should consider buying a small ranch for herself.

Sarah liked her condo. It suited her, and she had plenty of closet space—especially with the new closets she had built into the spare room. But she did love the "out west" aspect of living on a ranch. It's one reason that she loved to go to the old Red Bluff. She had realized that a few weekends before. It was the whole atmosphere—the feeling—of being there. And that was the same reason that she had originally joined the Victorian Society in town—a group of men and women who dressed up in Victorian clothing and attended various events around town celebrating—ironically—the old Red Bluff. The feeling of living in the old west had always thrilled her.

Sarah had often said that she was born in the wrong century. She and Jenna used to talk about that. Jenna felt the same way. Now, Jenna was back in the nineteenth century living the good life. While Sarah was here, alone with a dreary job.

Dancer danced to the side of the trail, jarring her out of her reverie. That's why she had named him Dancer— he always danced this way and that—at real or perceived noises. This time it was a bird in the underbrush. Sometimes just the sound of the wind scared him. But Sarah didn't mind. She liked her horses with spirit, just how she liked her men.

Not that spirited men had ever worked out for her. Marcus wasn't the first spirited and powerful man that she had fallen for. Her boyfriends in high school and college had always been president of the student body or had some other position of power. And her relationships with them had always ended badly. After graduation, more of the same.

That thought brought her a brief pang of regret. Carl. "Carl the CEO" is what she called him after their divorce. Carl, who was CEO of his own company and on the board of directors of several important organizations in town when he was twenty-four years old. When he asked her to marry him, she thought she was the luckiest woman in the world. Rich, handsome, powerful, Carl had it all. He also had an insatiable desire for other women, which Sarah found out the hard way after five blissful months of marriage. At least she thought they were blissful. Until the day she visited him at the office unannounced and found him in passionate embrace in the copy room with his new bosomy secretary. Broken-hearted, she filed for divorce that afternoon. Exactly five months to the day from when they were married. It took her months to recover.

Dancer turned onto the trail that led to the cave. Sarah took a deep, relaxing breath. As they entered the cave, she realized that it wasn't just the old west atmosphere that she liked about the old Red Bluff. When she walked through this cave and emerged into another world—the world of 1870—it felt like she had left all her mistakes behind. She felt washed clean. And that was a good feeling.

CHAPTER TWO

MATTHEW SMILED WHEN he thought of Sarah James and that he would see her soon. When she first walked into his saloon several months ago, it was like his life had started anew. He felt as if he had been living under a dark cloud for the past three years, and Sarah had brought sunshine back into his life.

Three years ago. Matthew sighed. Had it already been three years since Catherin had died? He moved his head slowly from side to side. Such a long time. So much grief. It had been Catherin's idea to move west, so he didn't feel at all responsible for her death. He had been content to stay where they were. Missouri was home to him, and he had no reason to leave. But Catherin had wanted the adventure of moving out west. And now she was gone. Several other people on the wagon train had also died of dysentery on the long trip west. So, he hadn't been alone in his grief when it happened.

Then he had stopped in Red Bluff the same time as Josiah Stone had become sheriff. Josiah wanted to clean up the town. Besides getting rid of the rowdies having gunfights in the street, he had emptied the place of the,

6

um, previous occupants. Josiah said that everybody had a right to make a living, even *those* women, but not in his town. The owner of the saloon—it wasn't called a saloon back then—wanted to make a quick sale and leave with his women, so he sold it to Matthew at a good price; and Matthew turned it into a saloon. The piano—what drew Sarah James here to begin with—had come with the place.

Matthew didn't feel bad about not grieving anymore. Before she died, Catherin had told him that she wanted him to move on and be happy. But the grief had been with him for so long that he felt as if there was a missing piece in his life. And he knew who that missing piece was. Sarah.

It wasn't just that she was so lovely. Her voice melted his heart. She sang for tips only, and lately he had been passing around a glass at the bar trying to get her extra tips. If he was unsuccessful at that, he would take tips out of his own tip glass to put into hers. Matthew had noticed that Sarah became especially excited when she saw a dollar gold piece in her tip glass, so he always managed to give her at least one.

And every weekend that she came to sing at his saloon, he felt himself falling deeper and deeper in love with her. Of course he hadn't told her. He wouldn't tell her. It was enough for him to enjoy her voice and her beautiful smile from afar. An occasional touch. She often touched him as they talked. Matthew lived for those moments.

But he wouldn't say anything about his feelings for her. He wasn't like that. Matthew Pelletier knew himself well. And just as he knew that he would have been forever content to be in someone else's shadow in Missouri—as a printer's apprentice—he knew he would not be the one to make his feelings known to Sarah James.

Although he knew that some men—well, most men—were adept at going after women, Matthew knew that he wasn't one of those men. Catherin had proposed to him. If she hadn't, he knew they never would have ended up together. Catherin must have known that, too. He had loved her quietly since she first crossed his path. As usual, he had said nothing. He was polite. He tried not to stare. But he loved her with his whole being. And when she finally did propose, he had grabbed her into his arms and kissed her. Matthew smiled to himself. He still remembered her reaction.

"So is that a yes?" Catherin had asked.

In answer, all he could do was kiss her again. She smiled at him, kissed him back, and said, "I suppose that is a yes."

Matthew smiled as he washed the glasses from the night before. He wasn't in a hurry for anything. Everything got done when it got done. There were two kinds of people in the world: people who made things happen, and people who things happened to. Matthew was content to be the latter. So he would continue to enjoy Sarah's voice and enjoy gazing at her beauty. If she wanted him, she would make it known. If not, he was content the way it was.

The saloon doors swung open, and sunshine poured in. That is, *his* sunshine. Sarah had arrived from wherever it was she came from. She still hadn't told him where that was. And he felt satisfied to wait until she did.

CHAPTER THREE

AFTER OPENING THE swinging doors of the saloon, Sarah set down her bag. This was her routine every week. Leave her bag at the saloon, and then take Dancer to the livery stable. Although she could have as easily dropped it inside the front door of the hotel, which was across the street, she always felt more comfortable dropping it at the saloon.

She smiled at Matthew. He was so kind to her. So kind *and* so handsome! It was too bad he wasn't her kind of guy. If he was president of the town or something, maybe. But merely the owner of the local saloon? Not really her cup of tea.

Giving him a quick wave, she backed out the door and rode her horse to the livery around the corner. After dropping Dancer off, she walked back, swinging her arms and smiling. When she stepped into the saloon, she felt enveloped in warmth. Like it was exactly where she was meant to be. Sarah loved the feeling. It wasn't just the singing and the appreciation that she received for her singing that drew her to this time and this place. It was that feeling of warmth she experienced in that saloon. A strange place for a feeling like that, she thought. But it was real. She felt it every time she walked through that door.

She looked up to see Matthew looking at her. She smiled at him again, grabbed her bag, and said, "Be right back, Matthew!" before heading back out the door.

Sarah walked across the street and into the hotel. Eliza, the owner of the hotel, greeted her warmly as she always did.

"Hallo, dear. Did you have a good week back home?" asked Eliza, as she smiled at Sarah and handed her the key.

Sarah smiled back. "It was a good enough week, Eliza. Not as good as here, though!" said Sarah.

Eliza was one of the only locals who knew exactly where Sarah really came from. That made Sarah feel close to her. She took her key and walked upstairs to her usual room. After putting her bag down on the bed, she looked around. Eliza always gave her the same room, so it was almost like home. The bed, the dry sink with the bowl of water and the pitcher, the chamber pot in one corner and the small wood stove in the other corner. When she was here, about the only thing she missed was having a real bathroom. But she had gotten used to it, and it wasn't such a hardship anymore.

Sarah walked down the stairs, across the street, and back into the saloon. She sat down at the bar. Matthew had a sarsaparilla already poured for her.

"Thank you, Matthew!"

"Nice to see you again, Sarah," said Matthew. "How's your week been?"

"Oh, same old crud."

"What did you say you did, again?" asked Matthew.

Sarah smiled at him in response. "Oh, that's right. I'm not supposed to ask those questions."

"Oh, you can ask."

Matthew laughed. "I can ask, but you won't answer, huh? Okay, if you don't like your job, why don't you come here and sing full-time?"

"Matthew, you don't pay me! I couldn't support myself on just tips. Besides, I have, you know, another life."

"Another life, huh? Anything that I should know about? Do you have a husband and family in your other life?"

Sarah laughed. "Not that much of another life! No husband, no family. Just a job I can't stand, and a place to live that is strictly mediocre."

"Ah, just a minute, Sarah. Be right back," Matthew turned away to pour beers for a couple of cowboys who had walked in.

One cowboy sidled up to Sarah. "Hello, beautiful. Want to come home with me, sometime?"

Sarah looked at him to size him up. He was another handsome specimen of nineteenth-century cowboy, but he looked fifteen years old. She wondered what the drinking age was in the nineteenth century or if they even had one.

"Dude! Does your mother know that you're not in school today?" asked Sarah.

The cowboy's smile drooped. He took the beer from Matthew and tromped over to his buddy who was already sitting at a table.

"You're good at putting off those cowboys, Sarah! Let's see, where were we? Oh, yes, your mediocre job and place to live. If it's that bad, why don't you stay here full-time? Is your 'other life' that important to you?"

Sarah noticed that Matthew's eyes sparkled. He was an attractive man. Too bad he wasn't more her type of guy, because she could really go for him. She liked the way he made her feel.

"Now, that you mention it, Matthew, it's not that important. I don't know why I insist on staying, but I do. Until I figure out why, I'm going to keep doing what I'm doing."

"Even though you're unhappy?"

Sarah tilted her head when she answered. "I'm happy! What makes you think that I'm not?"

"Because when you talk about your other life, you look sad, Sarah. That's all."

"That's only because I'm so happy when I'm here!"

"That's why I think you should stay!"

"Where would I stay? Is there another ranch around like Jenna bought?" Jenna, Sarah's best friend, had just married Josiah, who was Matthew's best friend. "Even if there was," continued Sarah, "I'd have to ride home late at night, and I wouldn't like that."

"You could stay here."

"Here? Where? Sleep in the bar?" laughed Sarah.

"No, Sarah, I wouldn't suggest that! Not even Rawlins sleeps here!" Matthew referred to the town drunk, also the deputy sheriff, who was now in the corner with another bottle and close to passing out.

"Then where do you mean?" asked Sarah.

"I have rooms upstairs."

"I thought *you* lived up there."

"I do. I converted several rooms into a two-bedroom place for Zack and me. But there are still other rooms up there. Would you like to see them?"

"Sure. I don't have to start singing for a while."

"Zack! Zack! Can you watch the bar for me? I'll be right back. I'm going to show Sarah the rooms upstairs."

"Sure, Matthew. I've got it," said Zack. "Will you be staying here with us, Sarah? Instead of going home every week?"

"Just thinking about it, Zack. Nothing's for sure yet." Sarah liked Zack. He was a kid who lost his parents, and Matthew had kind of adopted him. Kid isn't the right word. Zack was twenty-two. He was more like a little brother to Matthew, who had been looking after him for years.

"Oh, I wish you were staying, Sarah. We all love hearing you sing!"

"Thanks, Zack," she said, as she followed Matthew up the backstairs.

CHAPTER FOUR

"HERE'S THE FIRST one, Sarah," said Matthew, as he opened the door.

She peered into it, and it resembled her hotel room across the street. Bed, wooden sink with a bowl and a pitcher, a chamber pot in one corner, and a small wood stove in the other. "Looks the same as my hotel room."

"The other two empty rooms are the same. You want to see those?"

"Sure."

Matthew opened the door to the next one. Sarah looked into it, and it was the same as the first. The third one was the same, also.

"What's down there?" Sarah asked when she saw two more doors.

"That's where I live. Would you like to see it?"

"Yeah, I'd like to see where you hang out."

"Where I what?" He tilted his head and looked confused.

"Oh, sorry. Where you live," Sarah smiled to herself. She reminded herself: when in the nineteenth century, talk like someone in the nineteenth century!

14

Matthew opened the door, and Sarah followed him in. A large wood cookstove stood in the center of the room. The kitchen area was to the right of the cookstove and had a table and four chairs. To the left was a sofa, chair, and side table. On the outside wall was a fireplace. On the mantel was a picture of a beautiful, young woman. To the left of the room were two doors, each leading to a bedroom.

"Why do you have a fireplace *and* a wood stove?"

"I like to watch the fire. Sometimes I can sit in front of it and gaze for hours."

"Me, too! I love watching the flames. Who is the woman in the picture?"

Matthew walked over to the picture and picked it up. He traced the woman's face with his finger. "This was my wife, Catherin. She died in the wagon train on the way out here."

Sarah put her hand on his arm and squeezed it gently. "I'm so sorry, Matthew. I didn't know."

"It's all right. It's been several years now. I'm ready to move on."

"You mean, be with someone else? But you haven't, right?"

"I'm waiting for the right woman to ask me!" Matthew grinned at her.

"Ask you what?" asked Sarah, confused.

"To marry her!"

"Men should do the asking."

Matthew glanced at the picture that he had replaced on the mantel. "Some women ask. She asked me."

"Matthew, you're so cute!" Sarah pinched his cheek as you would a baby. "You might be waiting a long time for another woman to do that. She's," Sarah nodded toward the photograph, "beautiful *and* unusual. Most women want the man to ask."

Matthew took a step closer to her. "And you, Sarah, what do you want?"

Uncomfortable, Sarah stepped away. "I want to go downstairs and sing!"

"It's still early."

"Late enough. I'll give those cowboys some extra bang for their buck today."

"Some what?"

"Oh, sorry, some extra songs." Sarah, she told herself, you need to be more careful with your speech. She walked out the door, and Matthew followed.

"So, do you think you'd want to stay in one of these rooms?"

"The rooms you showed me have no place to cook. I could stay there instead of the hotel. But as far as living there full-time, I don't think it would work out. How would I cook my meals?"

"I'd cook 'em for you."

"Oh, I couldn't ask you to do that, Matthew."

"Why not? I cook for Zack and me. I make plenty for three people anyway. It wouldn't be any extra work for me."

"And how much would this queenly treatment cost me —for the room and my meals?"

"I'm not paying you. So you sing every night or most every night, and you get the room and meals free! That's fair, isn't it?"

"That's nearly an offer I can't refuse, Matthew! Let me think about it. I don't know what I'd do with my con— the place I live. I'd have to sell it or something." She knew he wouldn't know what a condo was, but at least she stopped before saying the whole word. "And quitting my job would be a huge decision. Give me some time."

CHAPTER FIVE

MATTHEW WALKED DOWN the stairs behind her. He loved the way her hips moved. If truth be known, he loved everything about her. Now he had the whole evening to enjoy her beautiful voice. And just looking at her gave him more pleasure than he could hope for. Although he'd love to have her living here, he didn't know if he could handle it. This way, he had the whole week to recover himself before he saw her again. He sighed and walked behind the bar. But he'd like to try.

"Thanks, Zack," said Matthew.

After he poured whiskey for two cowboys who had just come in, he walked to the corner of the bar that was closest to the piano—and Sarah. Leaning down, he rested his chin in his open hands and concentrated on her voice and her beauty. Did she know how in love with her he was? How could she not know? He smiled as she sang one of his favorite songs, "Scarborough Fair." When she glanced over at him while she sang, he winked at her, which made her smile.

"Barkeep!"

Something coming from the side sounded familiar to

Matthew, but he was too consumed in watching and listening to Sarah to pay it much mind. He sighed and closed his eyes momentarily to feel the impact of her song. There was nothing like her singing. Nothing like it in the world.

"BARKEEP!"

Matthew opened his eyes and stood up straight. Turning to the right, he saw the cowboys' glasses were empty.

"Oh, sorry," he said, as he poured more whiskey.

"She's beautiful and has a nice voice," said one cowboy. "Is she your woman?"

Matthew looked over at her and smiled. "Not yet," he said, as he returned to his place at the corner of the bar.

Sarah's next song was "Buffalo Gals," and Matthew always enjoyed hearing that one. With a broad grin on his face, he turned back to see if the cowboys needed more whiskey. They had moved to the poker game at the table by the window. Zack would take care of them now. So he could focus all his attention on Sarah.

"Chief! More whiskey!" a cardplayer called. Matthew hated it when they called Zack "chief" just because he was half Indian. Of course that was better than some other names they called him. He wished he could do something about it, but he didn't know what. Kick them out of his saloon? Then he wouldn't have much business, because almost everyone called Zack some insulting nickname.

Zack took the abuse well. Matthew wasn't sure if that was good or not. But Zack said it didn't bother him, so Matthew had to accept it. He knew Zack wanted to leave town—his dream was to go to college. What chance of that did he have? Poor kid. When Zack returned to his seat in the corner with his book, Matthew returned his attention to Sarah.

Ah, Sarah. He could spend the rest of his days on this earth just watching her and listening to her sing. This was his heaven right here. He didn't need anything more.

After a few more songs, Matthew noticed that Sarah's glass was almost empty, so he filled it with more sarsaparilla. She kept the glass on the table next to the piano. Sarah loved the piano and didn't want to put any glass with liquid on top of it. The table hadn't been there when Sarah first started playing in the saloon; Matthew had moved it there for her convenience.

He'd do anything for her, to make her more comfortable, to make her happy, maybe to convince her to live here full-time. Matthew didn't know where she came from, but he suspected she might be rich. He had noticed that she had never worn the same dress twice. Most women here had two, maybe three dresses if they were lucky. But Sarah had an endless supply of them. Where did she come from that was close enough to ride her horse to in one day? He knew it was one day, because on Sundays, she would often say something about work the following day. Wherever it was, he prayed that she'd keep coming back here to Red Bluff.

CHAPTER SIX

WATCHING MATTHEW WATCH her as she sang gave her an eerie feeling. A good feeling. Who wouldn't feel good with a good-looking hunk of a man unable to take his eyes off her? Other men in the saloon watched her. But the way Matthew looked at her was different. It was like he cared. She liked it. She liked him. It was too bad that he wasn't her kind of guy.

She finished for the evening, and while she was taking her last sip of sarsaparilla, she saw Matthew with a tip glass in his hand going around from table to table saying, "For the singer! For the singer!" Sarah enjoyed seeing him do that, and he always had such a look of accomplishment on his face when he poured his glass of coins into hers.

Oh! Two gold coins this time. With a haul like this, maybe she *could* consider quitting her regular job. Maybe she *should* consider it. Since she had stopped being in love with her boss, Marcus, she had realized things about the job that she hadn't noticed before.

Like him asking her to pick up his dry cleaning. She used to feel honored when he asked her, as if it was something personal that he was sharing with her. But recently, she had realized that he was asking because she was his employee. Period. He didn't want to burden his loving wife with his boring cleaning, so he asked "the help" to pick it up for him. Sarah was tired of being the help. Quitting her job was sounding better and better all the time. As she fell asleep in her hotel room that night, she was studying the possibility of leaving her job.

She awoke the next morning feeling happy and refreshed. Of course, she always woke up in the old Red Bluff feeling happy. That was in contrast to waking up in her own Red Bluff dreading going to work. What would it feel like to wake up happy every day? How wonderful that would be. And that possibility was now within her reach.

Sarah dressed and walked over to the livery stable. Ezra, who ran the place while his father worked next door as blacksmith, had Dancer already saddled and waiting for her. She had remembered to ask him yesterday, and it worked out perfectly.

She mounted Dancer and rode out of town toward Jenna and Josiah's ranch. Jenna had invited her for breakfast and to show her all the improvements to the ranch that her brother Ryan had accomplished. Improvements equaled modernizing. The first improvement was to replace the outhouse with an indoor composting toilet. No one could expect a "modern" girl from 2014 to use an outhouse all the time—especially in the winter.

As Sarah rounded the bend, she saw another of Ryan's improvements. He had built a small corral around the barn, so the horses didn't have to stay in their stalls all day. Eventually he would build a fence around the surrounding pasture.

Sarah smiled as she turned Dancer loose in the corral with Magic. She missed the daily chitchat that she and Jenna used to share. If she did decide to live here full-time, she would have that pleasure again. Well, sort of. There were no phones here, so it wouldn't be every day once Jenna and Josiah moved to their ranch. Today was a treat. Jenna was here making changes and making it into a home. But every night she went "home" to Josiah at the sheriff's office. When he found a decent deputy, Josiah would be free to come home at night, and then they'd move here full-time. The deputy he had now wasn't even close to being decent. He spent his days drinking and his nights sleeping in a cell at the jail. Jenna jokingly referred to the drunk deputy as her "roommate."

"Sarah!" Jenna called from the doorway and rushed out to meet her friend. They hugged, and Jenna invited her inside. "Come see the new bathroom!"

Jenna led Sarah into the larger of her two bedrooms. There, along the wall in the corner of the room, Ryan had built another small room. Inside was a dry sink with the bowl and pitcher, and a square wooden box with a toilet seat attached to a hinged top. A toilet paper holder was attached to the wall, and a towel hung above the sink.

Jenna started to open the lid of the toilet and said, "Do you want to see how it works?"

"No, no," said Sarah. "Too much information! Is it working, though? Can I use it?"

Jenna laughed. "Sure, Sarah, go ahead. And see here, real toilet paper! We could have bought a solid plastic composting toilet, but Josiah insisted that we keep it looking like the present instead of the future. He said that he doesn't want the world to know that he married a girl from the future. Of course, he didn't complain when I insisted on toilet paper. Anyway, there you go."

She came out of the bathroom and said, "Much nicer than an outhouse! Thank you!"

"Come on in and sit down," said Jenna.

Sarah looked around the room. "I still can't believe you bought all this beautiful furniture for twenty-five dollars!" She sat down and said, "It's pretty comfortable, too. So are you still happy here, Jenna? Do you miss being in the future?"

"Not at all. There are some modern conveniences that I miss, of course, and some people, but that's all. Ryan is finally all moved into his place, and my sister Kat has visited a few times. And since Granny married Edward and moved here, it's almost like home. Well, it *is* home."

"How is everything going with Josiah? Are you still madly in love?"

Jenna nodded her head. "More than ever. He is the most wonderful man that I've ever been with. He spoils me in so many ways. Of course, I spoil him, too!" Jenna and Sarah both laughed. "How about you, Sarah? How are you doing?"

The smile faded from Sarah's face, and she slowly shook her head. "I hate my job. It feels like I hate it more and more every day. Now that I'm not in love with Marcus anymore, lots of things he does irritate the hell out of me. I can't stand when he wants me to pick up his dry cleaning!"

"You used to love that!"

"Yes, I know. That's how much everything has changed for me. I dread going to work every day. All day long, I watch the clock and can't wait to get home. Once

I get home, I start dreading going in the next day. The only time I'm at peace is when I'm here."

"You know what that sounds like to me, Sarah?"

"What?"

"That you need to move here!"

"That's what Matthew keeps telling me. Yesterday, he showed me some rooms above the saloon. He said I could stay there free, and he would even cook my meals for me!"

"So you two haven't . . . " Jenna raised her eyebrows toward Sarah.

"No! Of course not! He's not my type at all! You know that. I like leader-of-the-pack type men."

"Yes, I know, but that hasn't gotten you very far. Maybe it's time for a shift in thinking. A shift in time and a shift in thinking! Ha!"

"Matthew's nice, but he isn't my type."

"He's *very* handsome."

Sarah shrugged and looked away uncomfortably. "I'm hungry. I thought we were having breakfast."

Jenna stood up and said, "Oh, yeah! I almost forgot!" Then she retrieved a cast-iron skillet from a cabinet in the kitchen and set it on the wood stove. "I did remember to get the stove going, though." She peered inside. "It must be ready. I still don't have this down yet, so if I mess it up, we'll go to Eliza's for breakfast!"

"I'm sure you'll do fine, Jenna."

Jenna spooned some lard into the pan, moved the pan around while it melted, then put the eggs in and dropped some already peeled and shredded potatoes in beside the eggs. While they were cooking, she lay a piece of tinfoil on the top of the wood stove and placed four pieces of bread on top of it.

"Tinfoil? That doesn't sound like 1870s to me." said Sarah.

Jenna laughed. "What Josiah doesn't know about won't hurt him! Besides, I think it came into use in the late 1800s, anyway."

They ate their breakfast, and Sarah kept raving over how well Jenna had done using the wood stove and the cast-iron frying pan.

"You can get used to anything, I think," said Jenna. "Especially when there is something that is even more important to you."

The two women talked all afternoon about old times, new times, old Red Bluff and new Red Bluff. Jenna told her how happy Ryan is to be here, and how in love Granny and Edward are. "They can't keep their hands off each other! It's so cute!"

Finally, late in the afternoon, Sarah looked out the new window glass that Ryan had installed and said, "Oh, no! It's gotten so late! I'll be late for my job!"

"Sarah, it's volunteer work—you don't get paid to sing!"

"Yes, but Matthew is expecting me, and I can't let him down. Bye!" She hugged Jenna, ran out to the corral, grabbed Dancer, and hurried down the road. With Dancer knowing which way home was, she didn't have to ask him to hurry.

26

CHAPTER SEVEN

THAT MORNING, MATTHEW had awakened with a smile. He had just finished a dream about Sarah, and still had the taste of her on his lips. He looked forward to spending the afternoon with her and then listening to her sing all night. That's what he looked forward to all week long. And after tonight, he'd have to wait another week to see her.

Unfortunately, he still hadn't persuaded her to move here. Matthew had offered her the room free and had offered to cook her meals. What else could he do to convince her to move here? She wasn't happy with her job—whatever it was. So why was she resisting? Somehow, he had to get her to move here. His life wasn't the same when she wasn't around.

Midafternoon, Matthew started watching the door. Usually, Sarah would have been there already. She'd sit at the bar, and they would talk until it was time for her to sing. Matthew wasn't sure which meant more to him—listening to that beautiful voice of hers, or the conversation at the bar. Probably the conversation. When she sang, she could belong to anybody. But when they talked at the bar, he had her complete attention. It was like she was already his.

As the afternoon wore on, Matthew became more and more nervous. Sarah should have been there. Where could she be? He didn't plan to wait much longer before seeing if Eliza knew where she was. He hoped she wasn't hurt or anything. If she lived here, this wouldn't happen, thought Matthew.

No! What was he thinking? He was kidding himself. If she lived here, he still wouldn't always know where she was. Not unless they were together. Not unless she was his. He had to figure out a way to make that happen. This waiting for her to show up whenever she pleased was starting to annoy him. It wasn't that he wanted to possess her. It was that he wanted to share in her life—to be a part of her life. Because she was rapidly becoming all of his.

Another hour crawled by. Matthew could barely serve drinks because he was so focused on the swinging doors. No sign of Sarah, yet. Finally, he walked out the door and looked up and down the street. Nothing. He came back into the saloon and walked to where Zack was sitting at a back table, reading.

"Zack, can you watch the bar? I'm going to walk over to the livery and see if Sarah's horse is there."

"Sure thing, Matthew." Zack stood up and walked behind the bar.

Matthew hurried out the door and down the street. Taking another look up the street to make sure she wasn't approaching from behind, he turned the corner and half ran to the livery stable. Ezra had disappeared somewhere, so Matthew walked down the aisle looking for Sarah's horse. It wasn't there. A quick check of the corral outside showed it wasn't there, either.

He rushed back to the saloon and peered in. Thinking maybe she could be in the outhouse in the back, he called inside, "Zack? Sarah?"

Zack shook his head as he poured a whiskey for someone at the bar. "Haven't seen her, Matthew."

Matthew crossed the street trying to calm himself down and tell himself that she was fine and there was nothing to worry about. Opening the door of the hotel, he stepped in and called out for Eliza.

"Yes? Oh, hallo, Matthew. How are you doing this fine afternoon?" As she stepped closer and saw his worried expression, she said, "Matthew, are you all right?"

"It's Sarah," said Matthew. "She's really late today. Do you know where she is? Do you think she's okay?"

Eliza put her hand on Matthew's arm. "I'm sure she's fine, Matthew. No need to worry. She went off to Jenna's ranch this morning for breakfast. I'm sure they just got carried away with talking. She'll probably be here any time now."

Matthew inhaled deeply and realized that he hadn't been breathing. He looked down at the floor and then back at Eliza. "Okay, thanks, Eliza. I've been worried about her. I don't want anything to happen to Sarah."

"I can see that, Matthew." Eliza nodded her head, then checked out the window. "Look! There she is now."

Matthew turned abruptly, opened the door, started heading out, and then turned around quickly. "Thanks, Eliza!"

Sarah had stopped her horse in front of the saloon and was dismounting when Matthew rushed up to her.

"Sarah!" he said, as he approached her. He held out his arms but could not manage to embrace her. "I was so worried about you!"

"Oh, that's sweet of you, Matthew. I was at Jenna's and didn't realize how late it had become. Can you get Zack to take Dancer over to the livery for me? Thanks!" Sarah said, as she walked into the saloon and sat down at the piano.

Matthew took another deep breath. He put his hand over the horse's neck for support. "Let's go, big fella. I won't bother Zack. *I'll* take you over to the livery. I need to calm myself down." Matthew walked slowly toward the livery stable to give himself time to think.

He knew he was in love with Sarah. Of that much, he was certain. But these feelings of loss when she was just a little late, and the way she consumed his thoughts—it didn't make sense to him. He thought he had been in love with Catherin—no, he was sure of it, but he didn't remember these overwhelming, consuming feelings. Maybe something was wrong with him. He'd have Doc Mercer take a look just to be sure.

CHAPTER EIGHT

SARAH HAD NOTICED how Matthew's arms had opened as he hurried up to her—like he was going to hug her. But he didn't. And that look of relief on his face. Why? She wasn't that late! He did look genuinely concerned, though. Matthew was unlike any man she had ever met in her life. She wondered if all the old-time cowboys acted like that. Josiah, Jenna's old-time husband, wouldn't count. When he found out that Jenna was from the future, he tried to end their newly budding romance. Well, if Matthew did have feelings for her, maybe she should tell him where she's from, and that would be the end of it.

What about her feelings for him, she wondered. No! There were no feelings. None. Matthew was a good guy, who happened to be extremely attractive—but—and it was a big but, he wasn't her type. Not at all. She liked strong, authoritative men—men who walked all over her. Wait! Where did that thought come from? They didn't all walk all over her. Well, most did, but she overlooked it because she liked their strength so much. Sarah knew Matthew would never walk all over her. But could she see herself with a man like him? She didn't know. She just didn't know.

As Sarah was singing "Streets of Laredo," Matthew walked in the door, and she smiled at him. She had wanted Zack to take Dancer to the livery, not Matthew. But he had done it himself. What a sweetheart he was. Watching as he crossed in front of the piano going toward the bar, she noticed his tight body and cute butt.

When she finished the song, she took a sip of the sarsaparilla that Matthew had placed on the table beside the piano. He always did things like that for her. Kind things. He was a kind man. Could she say that about *any* of the men she had ever been with in her life? No. Definitely no. Some had treated her better, some worse, but none of them could ever be called kind in any way. Not that they were mean—just not kind.

After a few more songs, Sarah sat down at the bar with Matthew. Usually, she sang more before a break, but she had hurried back from Jenna's and needed some breathing time.

"So you worried about me, huh, big boy?"

Matthew looked down with a sad expression on his face. "I don't want anything to happen to you, Sarah."

"Thanks, Matthew. I appreciate that."

Matthew walked to the other end of the bar to serve a couple of cowboys. While he talked to them, Sarah thought about the possibility of living full-time in the old Red Bluff. She glanced at Matthew still talking to the cowboys. Maybe if she had someone to love here, it might be easier to decide. Then she realized she was looking at Matthew while having the thought of loving somebody. The idea of that bothered her, and she didn't know why. Time to sing!

Sarah began the next set with "Oh! Susanna." That was one of her favorite old-time songs. She had needed to do lots of research to find out which songs were popular in 1870. Most of them she'd never heard of. Some of those didn't have sheet music, so she often had to make up her own melody to go with the words. Sometimes someone would correct her, and then she'd know. Often, though, she sang the old songs that she already knew, like "Oh! Susanna."

She was in the middle of singing "Yankee Doodle" when she heard a cowboy at the poker table yell, "Breed! Come on, Breed, bring me more whiskey!" She glanced over at Zack, who was at the corner table reading. He was too engrossed in the book to hear the cowboy. "Breed! You lazy half-breed idiot! Get over here and gimme some whiskey!"

Sarah had had enough. She had heard men call Zack that too often and had done nothing about it. Standing up in the middle of the song, she walked over to the poker table and looked at the guy who had yelled.

She narrowed her eyes and said, "*Don't* call him that."

The cowboy, surprised, looked up and said, "Why not? That's what he is, ain't he? A lazy half-breed?"

"For one thing," Sarah said, fighting to stay calm, "he is not lazy. He is reading a book. Perhaps you don't know how to read a book, and that's why you're confused."

The cowboy plunked his cards down on the table and glared at her. "Lady, I don't know who the hell you are, but I'll call the breed whatever I please. And I don't think you're gonna stop me. When am I going to get some more whiskey? Damn it!"

"I'd be happy to bring you some whiskey, sir," said Sarah politely. She walked slowly up to the bar and grabbed a bottle of whiskey from the counter.

Zack had looked up when the yelling was going on and said, "Sarah, I'll bring it to him."

"No, Zack, I will." She walked up to the poker table, and the cowboy looked up and smiled.

"That's a good girl, now, pour my whiskey and shut up." He held out his glass.

Sarah smiled demurely, curtsied, and poured half a bottle of whiskey directly into his lap. "There, that's a double. You can pay at the bar," and she walked away.

The cowboy, shocked at first, pushed away from the table and looked at the spreading stain on his crotch. First he put his hands on his hips and just stared at her. Then his hand touched the handle of his gun. "Lady, I ought to—"

Sarah turned back to look at him. "Sir, I do believe you've had an accident. There is an outhouse out back next time you have to go," and she returned to the piano.

"Lady! Look at me so I can shoot you where you stand!"

Matthew called out from the bar, "Cowboy, get your hand off your gun and get out of my establishment. You are no longer welcome here." He held a long barreled rifle pointed straight at the cowboy's chest.

Grumbling, the cowboy grabbed his money off the table and stomped outside. The other men at the table, their eyes still wide with surprise at Sarah's defense of Zack, quietly went back to playing poker.

Zack walked up and said, "Sarah, thank you, but you didn't have to do that. They always call me that. I'm used to it."

"Zack, you don't deserve to be called names. Nobody does. I don't like it, and I won't stand for it." Zack took the whiskey bottle from Sarah and walked over to the poker table to see if anybody wanted more.

Matthew came over to the piano and looked at Sarah. "You know, Sarah, I should dock your pay for wasting half that bottle of whiskey." He was not smiling.

Sarah looked at him not knowing what to think. She took a sip of the sarsaparilla at the side table beside her. Then Matthew took something out of his pocket and dropped it into the tip glass on top of the piano. It was a gold dollar. He walked away. Turning back when he stepped behind the bar, he smiled and winked at her.

CHAPTER NINE

AFTER SARAH POURED whiskey in the cowboy's lap, the rest of the evening sped by. Matthew found himself filled with glee. He had never defended Zack. Maybe because he thought that Zack should stand up for himself. Maybe because Matthew just wasn't quarrelsome. In some ways, he felt bad about that. On the other hand, Matthew knew that he would not stand up for himself, either, so he wasn't going to feel guilty over not standing up for Zack.

That's why Sarah doing that thrilled him so. It was like she was his other half. They complemented each other. Her actions made him love her even more. If that were possible. If he had wanted to hug her after thinking something had happened to her, he really wanted to hug her after she stood up to that cowboy.

Even when the cowboy had his hand on his gun, she didn't back down. Although maybe that was because she didn't understand the seriousness of the situation. That cowboy wasn't from around here, and he could easily have shot her without a second thought. But Sarah didn't always realize the dangers of living out here in Red Bluff. That's why he worried about her so. Probably where she lived, wherever that was, wasn't as dangerous as it could be here.

A new thought clutched at his heart. Yes, Sarah did a great job at shutting up the dang cowboy. But if he was a scalawag as he appeared to be, he might come back to get revenge. He looked savage as a meat ax, and he might come back to get her. The thought gave Matthew the chills.

She needed him to take care of her. What happened with the cowboy was more evidence of that. Sometime, she was going to get herself in trouble and not be able to get out of it. That's why she needed him. Why couldn't she see it? He shivered when goose bumps traveled across his back and down both arms. He hated to think what might happen to Sarah. Matthew was determined to convince Sarah that she needed him to take care of her, protect her, comfort her when she needed it. But how could he convince her? He hadn't yet convinced her to stay in a room above the saloon. Maybe he could fix it up better for her.

The following morning before going downstairs, he took a look at the room closest to where he and Zack lived. What would make it more appealing to get Sarah to stay? The frayed bedcover had a stain toward the foot of the bed—probably from someone lying on it with their shoes on—and the curtains had a rip in them. He'd replace all of that. Nothing was too good for Sarah. The bowl in the sink had a chip in it. Maybe a bowl from another room was better. He'd check that. The rugs were dirty; he would have Zack wash those. Matthew thought cleaning up the place might help to convince her to stay.

Then he had another idea. Eliza! She knew Sarah and would probably know what Sarah would like. He'd ask

Eliza for help. Running down the stairs two at a time, Matthew opened the door of the saloon and pushed through the swinging doors. Walking across the street, he stepped into the hotel to look for Eliza.

"Hallo, Matthew," said Eliza from behind the front desk.

"Hallo, Eliza! Can you help me with something?" Matthew looked around the room to make sure no one else was around. Asking for help like this embarrassed him.

"Sure, what do you need?"

"Is Sarah still here?" Matthew had forgotten that Sarah might still be at the hotel.

"No, she always leaves early on Sundays."

"Eliza, I'm trying to convince Sarah to stay in a room above the saloon."

"Oh, trying to cut into my business, huh, Matthew?" said Eliza, jokingly.

"No, no, Eliza, sorry."

"I'm joking, Matthew. Go ahead with your question."

"I want Sarah to stay with me, because, because, well, did you hear what happened last night?"

Eliza raised her eyebrows and nodded her head. "Our Sarah doesn't always understand the dangers of living out here. The story scared me."

"Exactly!" said Matthew. "I want her close so I can protect her." He hesitated, looked away, and then looked again at Eliza. "And because I like her." It wasn't a lie, he did like Sarah, but he couldn't bring himself to tell Eliza that he was completely in love with her.

"Excuse me for saying so, Matthew, but instead of trying to get her to stay in one of your rooms, you should be asking her out to supper—court her!"

Matthew shook his head nervously. "I can't do that, Eliza. Even asking her to stay in one of my rooms was hard for me."

"Would you like me to invite both of you to supper? That worked for Jenna and Josiah."

"No, thank you, Eliza. I wouldn't be comfortable with that, either. But can you tell me what she might like in her room, so I can get her to stay there. At least she'll be closer to me."

"I'm sorry, but I don't know Sarah well enough to answer that question. Maybe you could ask Jenna. You know, she and Sarah come from the same place." Eliza said the words and looked away uncomfortably.

"That's a great idea, Eliza! Thank you!" Matthew waved as he disappeared out the door and down the street to the sheriff's office.

CHAPTER TEN

JOSIAH, THE SHERIFF, hadn't yet found a new deputy, so he and Jenna were still sleeping in his small room in the back. But he was at his desk when Matthew walked in.

"Hi, Josiah. Can I ask you a favor? Would you mind if I talked to Jenna about Sarah?"

Josiah gave Matthew a knowing look and smiled. "No, Matthew, I don't mind. She's not here right now, though. Dang rebel woman. She went out to the ranch to pick up a few things. I asked her not to, but she can be so stubborn! There's been a bunch of renegade Indians causing trouble not far from here. They haven't hurt anyone— yet—just general mischief, although they've burned down some houses and stolen some horses, but I didn't want Jenna out there alone.

"If you want to talk to her, I'd be much obliged if you'd ride out there and make sure she comes back with you. I'm sure she can tell you anything you want to know about Sarah. They've been friends for a long time."

"Thanks, Josiah, I appreciate it. I'll bring her back!" Matthew walked out the door, down the street, and back into the saloon. Zack was reading at the back table when

40

he asked him to open the saloon at noon. Then he charged out the back door and across to the livery to get a horse.

Matthew didn't have his own horse—didn't need one. He rarely left town, and when he did, he could easily rent a good horse from the livery. Ezra, who ran the livery, always gave him the kind of horse that he liked—quiet. Since he only rode occasionally, he wanted a calm horse that wasn't difficult to handle. The horse he now rode was like that. Calm and gentle.

Riding toward Jenna and Josiah's ranch, Matthew felt excited. He felt like he was getting somewhere with Sarah. At least in his preparations for Sarah.

As he rode up to the ranch house, he noticed the newly completed corral was empty. Wondering if Jenna had already left and he had somehow missed her, he dismounted and walked into the barn. Jenna's horse was in a stall. Maybe she didn't want him outside in case the renegades came calling. He left his horse in a stall, walked to the front door, and knocked.

"Matthew!" said Jenna when she opened the door. "What brings you out here to our humble abode?"

"Jenna, Eliza suggested that I talk to you . . . about Sarah. Can I come in?"

"Sure, Matthew, come on in. Sit down. Would you like some water or something?"

"No, Jenna, no, and I'm supposed to bring you back with me. I told Josiah."

"Oh, he's just an old worrywart!"

"A what?" asked Matthew.

"Oh, sorry. He worries too much. Just because *somebody* saw those renegades, doesn't mean they're coming here. But here I am gathering stuff that I don't want

41

stolen or destroyed, so I guess I'm as bad.

"What did you want to know about Sarah?" asked Jenna.

"Well, I, well, um, wanted to convince her to stay in a room above the saloon. And I'm trying to figure out how to get her to agree to that. I thought I'd replace the bedcover and the curtains, and have the rugs washed. What else can I do? What would Sarah like?"

"First, I know that Sarah has a mind of her own, and if she doesn't want to move up there, she won't."

"Oh," said Matthew, disappointed.

"Hmmmm," said Jenna, as if she was considering something. "Okay, yeah, well, come here."

Jenna led Matthew into the main bedroom and opened the door to the bathroom. "If you want to entice her to stay with you instead of at Eliza's, you could get one of these." She motioned toward the composting toilet.

Matthew looked at it and scratched his head. "What is it?"

"It's called a composting toilet. It's used instead of an outhouse—you know, so you don't have to go outside to the outhouse, and you don't have to use a chamber pot."

"Why?" asked Matthew, still confused.

"Because it's more *convenient*, Matthew, and women *like* convenient!"

"Well, I don't know," said Matthew, reluctantly.

"Matthew, you wanted to know how to get Sarah to stay in your rooms instead of the hotel. This is it. That's all I can tell you."

"You're sure this would make a difference?"

"I'm certain of it!"

"Where can I get one? I've never seen anything like

it."

"I'm not surprised at that at all! You can make it if you're handy with wood. Or you can talk my brother, Ryan, into making you one. He's probably going to have to carry them at the general store, once word gets out!" Jenna pulled the quilt off the bed, stuffed it into a bag, and handed it to Matthew. "Here. Would you mind bringing that to town for me?"

"Oh, no, of course not. Are you ready to leave?"

"Yes, I was all packed except for that. It still all seems silly to me, preparing for something that might never happen. But this isn't my time and I—"

"What?" said Matthew.

"Oh, I meant I'm new to this town, so I don't completely understand it yet," said Jenna. "You ready to ride back, or do you want to try the toilet?"

Matthew felt his cheeks go instantly hot. "No, um, I'm ready, let's go," and he sped out the front door.

CHAPTER ELEVEN

SARAH SAT AT her desk frowning. Here she was, back at work again and hating it. She hated the computer, the legal briefs, the depositions, and the subpoenas. Even her smartphone, which she normally loved, now annoyed her. Sometimes her mind was so focused on the nineteenth century that she found herself in the back parking lot of her office building searching for the outhouse, when the women's rest room was right across from her door. It wasn't that she liked using an outhouse. It was more like she had gotten so used to it, that it didn't feel like an imposition anymore. Although, after seeing Jenna's composting toilet, *that* would be a welcome improvement!

And her feelings about Matthew! They were totally inappropriate. How often did she need to remind herself that he was *not* her kind of guy? Maybe she needed to seek out some eligible bachelor who *was* her type of guy. Who would that be? There were plenty of guys in her office, mostly attorneys, and every one of them aggressive and hard-hitting. It's the kind of attorney that Marcus liked to have in his organization.

She decided that she would try to be more open. Since she had started working here and because she had fallen for Marcus immediately, she had declined all advances. Now that she had emotionally pulled away from the Marcus fantasy, maybe they would try again.

Just then, a handsome attorney stopped in her doorway. She smiled broadly at him. Ah, this is a good start, she thought.

"Sarah, is Marcus here?" he asked.

"No, he's in court today."

"If he gets back and wonders where I am, can you tell him that I had to leave early to take my wife to the doctor? You know, she still has that foot problem going on and can't drive."

"Sure, I'll tell him," said Sarah, her smile drooping. Oh, yeah, she remembered, he got married last year.

Disappointed, she plodded to the break room to get more coffee. She didn't want to be here, and it was starting to affect her work. Pouring the coffee, she looked up when someone walked in the room. She listened as he talked on his cell phone.

"Sure, no, really, I understand. We'll do it some other time. No big deal. Sure, talk to you later. Bye."

He looked up and noticed Sarah at the coffee machine. "Hey, Sarah. How's it going? Haven't seen you around for a while."

"Hey, Chad. I've been here. Always here."

Chad stood next to her and poured himself a cup of coffee. "Sarah, why don't you let me take you out to dinner tonight? I know you always say no, but why don't you give me a chance? It will be a nice dinner, I promise."

Sarah smiled at him and said, "Yes, Chad, I would like

that."

Chad suggested they meet at the restaurant at six o'clock. Sarah agreed and walked back to her desk smiling. Perfect, thought Sarah as she sat down at her desk. Chad was attractive, charming, and dynamic. He was exactly her type of guy. She could hardly wait until dinner, and she didn't mind the rest of the day at all.

Sarah arrived at the restaurant five minutes early. As she stood in the waiting room, she looked around and smiled. There were several people sitting and waiting for a table, and only one seat available. She didn't mind standing. After five minutes, she thought to herself, this isn't bad, I know he's busy. My kind of guy!

Good aromas from inside the restaurant wafted out to her. Sarah gently inhaled and wondered what delectable dish she would choose for herself. Maybe prime rib; she loved prime rib. Or maybe Chad would split some chateaubriand with her. That would be great.

When he finally arrived ten minutes late, he had his cell phone to his ear and nodded to her without a smile. After he got off the phone, it turned out that he hadn't made reservations, so he gave the hostess his name, and they sat at the bar to wait. When they were finally called for dinner fifteen minutes later, Sarah still had half a glass of wine, and Chad had gone through two glasses and was on his third.

It was an elegant restaurant. A single candle flickered on the dark corner table where they were seated. Trying to focus on the positive about Chad instead of the mounting negatives, she smiled and looked at her menu.

When the waitress came, instead of letting Sarah order for herself, Chad said to Sarah, "I eat here often, and I know what's good. I'll order for you." Then he ordered baked salmon for both of them.

It shocked Sarah so much that he would order for her without asking, that for a moment she didn't say anything. Then she said, "But, Chad, I don't like salmon."

He patted her hand. "Oh, you'll love this, darling. Don't worry." And then he continued talking about a big case he was working on that Sarah had no interest in. When dinner was served, as she picked at her salmon and ate the vegetables around it, Chad continued talking. Sarah realized that besides saying "hmmm" and "yes" she had not been included in the conversation at all.

Halfway through the meal, his cell phone rang. He picked it up to see who was calling and said, "I have to take this." Then he turned his back on her, but didn't leave the table, so she heard his end of the entire conversation.

"Yes, I understand. I said I'd be there, and I will," he said into the phone. Sarah noticed him look at his watch. "I won't be late, don't worry. See you. Bye."

He turned back to his meal, took one bite of salmon, and said, "Oh, I forgot something. Sorry." Then he picked up his cell phone, tapped out a text message, and sent it. Picking up his fork again, he put another bite of salmon in his mouth and said, "Where did I leave off? Did I tell you what I did in court?"

"Yes, I believe you did." Sarah had finished her vegetables, picked at the salmon, and was thoroughly bored by the company. She couldn't wait for the evening to be over.

Luckily, when the waitress came with the dessert menu, he said, "Hope you don't mind, Sarah, but I don't have time for dessert tonight. Another time, maybe?"

47

"Yeah, sure," Sarah said while nodding her head. No way, was what she was thinking.

They walked out of the restaurant, and when the valet brought her car, he leaned over to kiss her on the mouth. It was so unexpected that she didn't have time to even step back from it.

"It was great, Sarah. Let's do it again real soon," said Chad, as he walked away.

Sarah drove away thinking that if Chad was her kind of guy then she needed to get her head examined. What a jerk! What did she ever see in guys like that? Thinking back on the men in her life, she realized that this wasn't an isolated case. It wasn't that Chad was more of a jerk than the rest. It was that they had all treated her this way, and she was too blind to see it. What an idiot I am, she thought.

CHAPTER TWELVE

ALL DAY TUESDAY, work was so busy that she didn't have time to think about men or how unhappy she was with her job. Wednesday morning, she was still swamped. So focused on the computer work she was doing, she didn't realize someone was standing in her doorway until he spoke.

"Hey, Sarah," said Chad. "Great time last night. Shall we do it again Thursday?"

Sarah looked at him and slowly shook her head from side to side. "No," she said and turned back to her computer. Although she didn't look up again, she thought that he stood at the door for a while longer. Then, involved in her work again, she forgot about him and the distasteful experience from the night before.

Four o'clock came, and she could finally take a breather. She was caught up and had finished the morning's project. Marcus walked briskly in and stood in front of her desk.

"Sarah," he said. Reaching out with a stub in his hand, he asked, "Can you pick up my dry cleaning for me, please?"

Sarah scowled, took the stub, and said a clipped, "Yes."

Marcus, not normally the most observant fellow, said, "Well, Sarah, it's four o'clock. You might as well pick up the cleaning and then go home. You can bring the clothes in tomorrow."

Sarah looked at him and nodded. "Yes, okay. Marcus, I'd like to take the next two weeks off. Would that be possible?"

"It's a little sudden, but if you can find someone in the secretarial pool to take your place, yes, that would be fine. Whatever you want." With that, he turned and left.

Sarah sat silently at her desk and fumed. She'd had enough of picking up his dry cleaning. Even for an hour off, it wasn't worth the aggravation. She powered down her computer, grabbed the dry cleaning stub, and left the office.

In her car on the way to the cleaners, she smiled. Things weren't that bad. An hour off from the old grind, and she would use it to her advantage. And she didn't know where her asking for vacation had come from, but it was an enlightened idea. She smiled at the thought of returning to her beloved old Red Bluff and not having to leave for two weeks. Absolute heaven. And Matthew—

Finding a parking place right in front of the cleaners, she walked in quickly, just wanting to get it over with. She handed the stub to the attendant, and while she waited for him to bring her the clothes, Nick walked in. Nick was a cop in Red Bluff and was the best friend of Jenna's brother, Ryan. He had been to the old Red Bluff once, where he saved Josiah from getting shot in a gun-fight by tackling the guy with the gun.

"Hey, Sarah, how's it goin'? You still singing in Red

Bluff on the weekends?"

"Hi, Nick. Yup, sure am. I'm hating my job here so much that I'm thinking of moving to Red Bluff." Sarah knew that their conversation would sound confusing if anyone was listening, because they *were* in Red Bluff right now. Only Sarah and Nick knew they were talking about the old Red Bluff.

"Really? That's amazing. First Jenna, then Ryan, Granny, and now you're thinking of going, too. I've actually given it some thought—you know, Josiah is looking for a deputy."

"Well, Nick, why don't you do what I'm about to do? I'm taking a two-week vacation there to try it out and to see if I can handle it."

"That's a *great* idea, Sarah! When are you going?"

"The next two weeks! Once I decided, I didn't want to wait. I'm going home tonight and putting my condo up for sale!"

"Oh! You are serious about this." Nick hesitated and seemed to be thinking. "You know, taking a vacation over there is a great idea. I have some vacation time coming, and the chief owes me a favor. If I can get a couple of the guys to cover for me, I might do that myself! You usually leave Fridays, right?"

"Yes, in the afternoon. I get off early."

"If I can swing this, can I ride out with you? I've only been there once, and I'm not sure if I know the way. And I work early shift on Friday, so the time would be fine. I haven't been out to Jenna's ranch, though, since Madison's been living there. Would it be a problem with me leaving my rig there for a couple of weeks?"

"No, not at all. Madison's cool. And sure, you can ride out with me." The dry cleaning had come back, and

Sarah paid for it. "Will you let me know if you can arrange it or not?"

"Sure, Sarah. I hope to see you Friday! Bye!"

Sarah walked out the door, started her car, drove home, and immediately called the realtor about selling her condo. The following day she would stop at the realtor's office to sign the agreement. She wasn't delaying this at all. Now was the time to act.

CHAPTER THIRTEEN

MATTHEW COULDN'T BELIEVE the one thing that might make a difference to Sarah would be one of those weird toilets. But Jenna knew her better than anyone else in Red Bluff, and that was her advice. He wouldn't have time to make it himself since he had to watch the saloon. But Zack was good with his hands and had made some of the furniture in their apartment upstairs. Matthew hoped that Samuel, Eliza's husband, or Edward, Eliza's father, could watch the saloon while he and Zack talked to Ryan at the general store. So he walked across the street and into the hotel. Eliza stood at the front desk.

"Hi, Eliza. Do you think Samuel or Edward could help me out for a short time? I need to go see Ryan at the store, and Zack needs to come with me. So, I have no one to watch the saloon."

"Sure. Let me find out which one is more available, and I'll send him right over. Would that be all right?" asked Eliza.

"That would be perfect! Thanks, Eliza."

Fifteen minutes later, Samuel came through the swinging doors. "Hi, Matthew! Glad I could help out."

"Hi, Sam. It shouldn't be too busy right now, but I didn't want to keep the place closed up, either. We shouldn't be too long. Let me get Zack." Matthew called upstairs for Zack.

"Stay as long as you need to, Matthew. I'll be fine here, and it will be a change from the restaurant."

Zack and Matthew walked over to the Ralston General Store, named after Henry Ralston. Ryan, Jenna's brother, bought it from him, but didn't change the name.

As they walked by the front of the store, Matthew noticed a big "SALE!" sign in the window. As they walked in, Matthew looked around. It was a lot emptier than when Henry had the place. The aisles were much clearer without boxes full of various items lying on the floor.

"Hallo! Ryan!" called Matthew.

"Just a minute. Be right out," said a voice from the back.

Matthew walked around until he found what he was looking for. A pretty white bedspread for Sarah's bed. Then he found a set of curtains that would go with the bedspread perfectly. Not that he was a designer or anything, but they did look good together, and he hoped they would suit Sarah.

"Hallo, Matthew, Zack. Sorry for the wait. I was just finishing my latest painting. What can I do for you?" asked Ryan.

"I need one of those newfangled toilets like you made for Jenna," said Matthew.

Ryan laughed. "Oh no. Word's gotten out. Now everybody will want one!"

"Would you mind explaining to Zack how to make one? He's good with his hands, and I don't have the time

54

right now."

"Sure. No problem. It's not difficult at all."

"Great." Matthew held up the bedspread and curtains. "Also, could you put these on my account. Plus any items Zack needs to make the dang thing."

Ryan laughed again. "I know, you don't understand what the big deal is. All I can say, Matthew, is that where we come from, everyone has one—or at least something close." He wrote down the two items that Matthew held. "And I'll get Zack fixed up with everything he needs. But why are you doing this, if I may ask?"

Matthew smiled. "A woman! What else?"

Ryan nodded and smiled. "It figures! It must be a woman who knows about these, though—Sarah?"

Matthew chuckled and nodded. Then he was out the door, leaving Ryan to teach Zack about newfangled toilets.

After replacing the bedspread with the pretty new one, Matthew replaced the curtains. Then he took the rug out back, hung it on the line, and started beating it. Since the rug had no stains, Matthew decided that beating all the accumulated dust and dirt out would be enough.

Later, while serving drinks at the bar, Matthew smiled when he heard Zack banging away out back on the newfangled toilet. He thought that he never would understand women, or why one would be so interested in such a strange gadget.

CHAPTER FOURTEEN

MATTHEW WAS AT the bar impatiently awaiting Sarah's arrival. He wanted to catch her before she ran across the street to the hotel. Wouldn't she be surprised! There was no way she could say no after the changes he made to her room. Was there?

He looked up as the saloon doors swung open. Sarah waved at him and disappeared back out the door before he had a chance to speak. Dang! After waiting and waiting and waiting, he couldn't believe he missed her like that.

A few minutes later, looking over the swinging doors, he saw her lead three horses past the saloon. Three horses? Why would she be leading three horses? That didn't make sense. He wondered whose horses they were.

A coldness stabbed him in the heart. A boyfriend! Sarah had a boyfriend, and that's why she didn't want to stay in the room upstairs. But whose was the third horse? That didn't make sense. Matthew began washing glasses, trying to calm himself down. There was no reason to be suspicious. If there had been just the two horses, maybe. But since there were three, he didn't think he had anything to worry about. He hoped.

When Sarah returned to the saloon, she glided up to the bar, gave Matthew a big smile, and said, "I feel great! Now! How about a sarsaparilla for your favorite singer?"

Matthew couldn't help smiling at her, but he noticed that she looked different. Her face was flushed, and she had a glow about her that he hadn't seen before. Maybe one of those horses *was* her boyfriend's. He hoped not. He'd show her the room and see what she said. Maybe he could determine that way why she looked like she did.

"Hi, Sarah," said Matthew, as he handed her the sarsaparilla. "I wanted to catch you before you went to the hotel. I'd like you to see how I fixed up the room for you."

"You don't give up, do you, Matthew? I wanted to stay there over the weekend, anyway. But yeah, let's go see the room." She took a long sip of her sarsaparilla and stood up.

Matthew led the way upstairs, and when he got to the door, he bowed down as he opened it, as if she were royalty. "Your highness."

Sarah laughed and walked into the room. It was the first thing she noticed. There in the corner, where the chamber pot had been, stood one of Ryan's composting toilets! She couldn't believe the difference in the room since the first time she had seen it. Matthew had cleaned the rug and replaced the curtains and bedspread. It was almost like home. She liked it.

"Oh, Matthew! You got me a composting toilet! I can't believe you did that for me! Thank you!" Sarah turned around, saw the big grin on his face, and hugged him.

He couldn't believe it. I guess Jenna was right, he thought. The feel of her body against his for those seconds made him want to grab her and kiss her. But he didn't want to scare her off, so he didn't. It looked like she would use the room!

"I'm so glad you like it, Sarah. I wasn't sure about that gadget, but Jenna said you'd like it, so I had Zack build one with Ryan's instructions. I'll go across the street now and get your bags."

Sarah shook her head. "No, I'm already checked in at the hotel. I want to stay there this weekend. But this is wonderful! Can I use the toilet now? Would you mind?"

Disappointed, Matthew still smiled and said, "Sure, Sarah." Then he backed out the door and closed it.

Walking down the stairs, he didn't know what to think. What did she mean this weekend? Did she mean that next weekend she'd stay here? And why did she want to stay there this weekend? To spend the night with her boyfriend? None of it made sense. Obviously, the best thing to do was to ask her. That just wasn't Matthew's way.

CHAPTER FIFTEEN

MATTHEW LOOKED AROUND and smiled. The saloon was humming tonight, and everyone enjoyed Sarah's singing. Her tip glass was almost half-full, and he had never seen it like that before.

Two tables were pushed together close to the piano to accommodate Josiah and Jenna, Nick, Ryan, Granny and Edward, Rachel, and Jenna's niece, Madison. Matthew knew that Nick was the guy who had saved Josiah from being shot—a second time—and then Josiah had asked him to be deputy. But this was the first time he'd been back since that day. Granny was Jenna's grandmother, and she had moved here and married Edward, who was Eliza's father. It was very confusing! Rachel was the new schoolteacher. And the way he understood it, Madison was here to visit Granny. The two extra horses that Sarah had led to the livery belonged to Nick and Madison.

Every chance he got, Zack would go sit next to Madison. They had met during Granny's birthday party a couple of months earlier. Matthew hated to keep calling the poor kid to work, but the saloon was so busy, he needed someone else to serve drinks.

Sarah, during her breaks, instead of coming to talk to him, sat at the table between Nick and Edward. That bothered Matthew. Although he had to admit that it was the only seat available at the table, except the one that Zack kept leaving whenever he was called to work.

Matthew noticed that a couple of cowboys at the far table needed refilling, so he called Zack. He didn't respond. Matthew called him again, and still nothing. The kid was deep in a spirited conversation with Madison. Finally, Jenna got up and came to the bar.

"Can I help?" she asked. "Madison is enjoying Zack so much, I'd rather not disturb them."

Matthew explained to her what to do and handed her the whiskey bottle. He watched as she walked over to the table and said something to the cowboys. They laughed. Oh good, thought Matthew, she's a natural. Then he had another thought, so he glanced over at the table to see if Jenna serving drinks bothered Josiah. But Josiah was conversing with Nick and didn't even notice. All was well.

As he poured more whiskey for the men at the bar, he looked at Sarah, sitting at the piano. She smiled and winked at him. He smiled back at her and watched her for a minute. She kept her eyes on him, and it felt like she was singing "Down in the Valley" just for him alone. Then someone caught his attention at the other side of the bar, and he missed watching her sing the rest of the song. She may not be staying in the room upstairs, but he still thought he had a chance with her.

CHAPTER SIXTEEN

SARAH HAD SPENT the morning chitchatting with Eliza and Granny. Nick was standing in for Josiah, which enabled Josiah and Jenna to spend the night at their own ranch for the first time. That's why Jenna wasn't around. And Madison, who had come to old Red Bluff to spend some time with Granny, left after a while to spend time with Zack at the saloon.

When Sarah had had enough girl-talk, she walked across the street with determination. She needed to explore the depth of her feelings for Matthew. Were the feelings only there because there was no one else in her life? Or were they real? That's what she needed to find out. She found him attractive, and he was so kind. And although she had thought he wasn't her type of guy, after the date with the jerk on his cell phone, she began to question her view of men.

What she had thought of as her type of men—strong, demanding, aggressive—were actually controlling, abrasive, and selfish. Well, at least the ones that she had fallen for—which said more about her than them. She felt certain that not all strong men were jerks. But those were

61

the ones she attracted and was attracted to. That was about to change.

For the first time in her life, she was doing *exactly* what she wanted to do: sing. And she loved doing it. She had never loved anything more. So maybe now she could allow herself to have a relationship with a man who treated her with kindness instead of disregard. A man like Matthew.

Sarah pushed through the swinging doors of the saloon and walked up to the bar. "Good afternoon, Matthew!"

He walked up, washing a glass as he spoke, and said, "Good afternoon, Sarah. So nice to see you. And you look beautiful today, as usual." Matthew rinsed the glass and put it on the back counter. Then he poured a sarsaparilla and put it in front of her. "For you, my lady," said Matthew, as he made a small bow.

Sarah laughed. "You better be careful, Matthew. If you keep treating me like that, you might not be able to get rid of me."

Matthew winked at her. "That's what I'm hoping," he said. Then someone came up to the bar whom he had to take care of.

She had already decided that she was not going to tell him beforehand that she would move into the upstairs room Sunday. For two weeks she would sing every night and enjoy Matthew's company every day. It would make her either love the life here or hate it. And she hoped, it would help her sort out her feelings for Matthew.

Sarah had also decided that before she allowed herself to fall for Matthew, she would tell him exactly where she was from. Jenna had not done that soon enough with Josiah, and it almost ruined their whole romance. Sarah would make certain that Matthew knew what he would be getting—a woman from the future—before their potential relationship went any further.

The question was, when would she tell him? Before she moved in upstairs? That would have to be tonight. Sarah didn't know if she was ready for that. She had just become accustomed to the idea of maybe being attracted to Matthew. Was she ready to make a confession like that so soon? Probably not. She should probably move in upstairs and see how everything progressed. There was plenty of time. Or she would let it happen spontaneously. When it felt right.

Before Matthew had finished serving drinks at the bar, Josiah and Jenna came in and sat down. Sarah walked over and sat with them.

"You two are frequenting the saloon a lot lately," said Sarah.

"Free time!" said Jenna. "With Nick taking over for Josiah, we have some free time together. It's awesome! Tomorrow, we're even going on a picnic!"

"That's great. I'm so happy for you two!" Sarah reached out and patted Jenna's hand.

Jenna leaned forward and said quietly, "Have you told Matthew yet?"

"Told Matthew what?" asked Josiah a little too loud.

Jenna shushed him and whispered in his ear, "Sarah is on vacation and staying upstairs here for two weeks."

"Oh, he'll be *very* happy when he finds that out," said Josiah.

"No, I haven't told him yet," said Sarah. "I'm going to surprise him tomorrow. And I also decided that I need to tell him where I'm from."

"Really?" asked Jenna.

"I think it's a *very* good idea," said Josiah.

Sarah pointed at Josiah and said, "See? That's why I'm going to tell him. He needs to know before he decides to get involved with me."

Josiah looked away and said under his breath, "Too late for that!"

Zack walked up to ask what he could bring them. Jenna ordered sarsaparilla, and Josiah ordered a beer. Sarah still had her sarsaparilla. When Zack walked away, Jenna said, "Sarah, do you want to come over Monday for breakfast again?"

"No, Jenna. I don't want you out there," said Josiah.

"Josiah, what difference does it make? We're sleeping there, now," said Jenna.

"I told you. Those renegade Indians aren't out at night. They only cause their trouble during the day."

Sarah thought about the "Indians." In the new Red Bluff, the term "Indians" was politically incorrect. And yet, if she called them "Native Americans" here, everyone would look at her like she was crazy. Or worse. While she was here, she reminded herself to go along with the crowd. Here, they were Indians. Back in the new Red Bluff, they were Native Americans.

Zack had walked up with their drinks. "I don't think they're Indians at all. I think they're pretending to be Indians."

Josiah looked at him. "What makes you think so, Zack?"

"Different things you've told me about them. They just don't sound like Indians," said Zack.

"But why would they pretend to be Indians?" asked Josiah.

"That's an easy one, Josiah." Zack frowned. "To cause

trouble for the Indians."

"That's not a bad theory, Zack. I'll keep that in mind," Josiah said and turned to Jenna. "I still don't want you going out there. Whoever they are, they're troublemakers. And I want you safe."

"Sarah and I will be together. We'll be fine, Josiah. Don't worry. Sarah, will you come over?"

"Sure, as long as Josiah doesn't get mad at me."

"No, Sarah, I won't be mad at you. I'll be mad at this stubborn woman that I married!" He grabbed Jenna and gave her a pretend shake. "I guess that's what I get for marrying someone," he lowered his voice, "who can vote!"

Sarah and Jenna both laughed.

CHAPTER SEVENTEEN

Matthew woke up Sunday morning, stretched, and frowned when he realized what day it was. Sarah would leave this morning without saying good-bye, as she usually did. She had probably already left by now. And it would be another week before he saw her again. He hated that. When could he convince her to stay here full-time? Matthew didn't know what Sarah's job was, but he knew she hated it. That was enough for him. Because he also knew how much she loved singing. You could see the passion in her eyes when she sang. You could feel it from across the room. There was no doubt that she loved singing. And if she loved it so much and hated her job back wherever she came from, why wouldn't she move here? He didn't understand that at all.

Later that morning, as he opened the main door of the saloon, he saw Madison riding her horse and waving to someone standing in front of Eliza and Samuel's hotel. Someone who looked a lot like—his heart gave a leap—it was Sarah! And she was still here!

He stood there, inside the swinging doors, watching her. Sarah kept waving until Madison was out of sight.

Then she stepped back into the hotel, but left the door open. A minute later, she came out again carrying her bag, followed by Samuel carrying two bags. She looked up, saw Matthew waving at her, and waved at him. His heart leapt again. She was headed in his direction!

"There you go. You can handle this from here, can't you, Matthew?" asked Samuel, as he set the bags on the floor.

"Sure, Sam. Thanks!"

Samuel walked back out the swinging doors and across the street. Sarah stepped up to Matthew, looked in his eyes, and said, "I hope that room you offered me is still available. I just happen to be in town for the next two weeks."

Matthew could hardly contain himself. He wanted to throw his arms around her, swing her around, and kiss her until he had no kisses left. But he couldn't do that. Instead, he said, "I've held it for you." Then he picked up two of the bags, headed for the stairs, and said, "Follow me."

When he put the bags down inside the room, he said, "How did you get these bags here?"

"I was going to have to make a few trips, but when Nick and Madison decided to come over, too, I asked them for help. It worked out perfectly! Don't you think?"

Matthew nodded his head. "Yes, perfect," he said.

Sarah put her hand on his arm. "Matthew, can I talk to you?"

"Sure."

"I mean, someplace we can talk in private. Not in the saloon."

"Oh, okay. How about our apartment? Zack isn't there right now."

"That's good."

Matthew didn't know why Sarah wanted to talk to him, but he hoped that it was something that he wanted to hear. He led the way and opened the door of his apartment to let Sarah in. They sat across from each other, and Sarah looked him right in the eye. He felt himself get his hopes up.

"I'd like to tell you exactly where I come from, before anything, um, happens between us," said Sarah. Matthew tilted his head and looked at her, but didn't say anything. "Did Josiah ever tell you where Jenna's from?" Matthew shook his head. He didn't understand why this was so important—why they had to be in private for this. "I don't come from anywhere around here," she said.

"So? That doesn't mean you can't move here."

"That's correct, I could still move here. But I need you to know where I come from. I need to tell you that now. I come from—" Sarah hesitated, "—the future."

"What?" said Matthew, confused.

"The year now is 1870, right?" asked Sarah.

"Yes," said Matthew, still confused.

"I come from the year 2014. It's still Red Bluff, but it's different. Everything is different."

Matthew smiled, but didn't mean it. He didn't know what else to do. "I don't understand what you're saying, Sarah."

"I'm not from your time, Matthew. I come from a future time. A time where they only use horses for pleasure not for transportation, a time when large metal objects, filled with people, fly through the air, a time that is more than a hundred years from now."

Matthew stood up and looked down at Sarah. "I don't know why you're telling me this, Sarah." He felt all-overish. He didn't like arguments, and this was as close to one as he wanted to get. This was information that he didn't want to hear, information that bothered him and made him want to hide. He didn't like this conversation, and it made him uncomfortable.

"Because I wanted you to know—thought you should know." Matthew stayed silent and looked at her accusingly. "Jenna is from there, too, and Granny, Ryan, Rachel, and Nick, too. All of us are from the future." He shook his head and started pacing the room. "Matthew," Sarah's voice showed signs of anxiety, "Josiah has been there, and so has Eliza."

"That doesn't make it any better," said Matthew.

"Matthew, I don't—I don't know what else to say."

"You don't have to say anything, Sarah. I need to think." He turned away from her, walked into his bedroom, and closed the door behind him. Not gently.

A few minutes later, he heard the outside door close. He thought Sarah had left, which gave him some relief, but instead he heard Zack's voice.

"Hi, Sarah! Where's Matthew?"

"In there," Sarah said flatly.

"Oh, okay. So, it's Sunday, and you're here! That's great! Does that mean you're going to sing tonight?"

"You know, Zack, I think I will be taking tonight off. I need to leave. Bye."

"Bye, Sarah, see you later," said Zack.

Matthew heard Sarah stumble from the room. He stayed in his room; he didn't want to talk to Zack or anybody else. He had to think.

CHAPTER EIGHTEEN

SARAH STUMBLED FROM the room, down the hall past her own room, down the stairs, and out of the saloon. She thought she should leave and go back to her own time, but she had planned to meet Jenna for breakfast the following day, and she didn't want Jenna to worry. In Sarah's distress, it never occurred to her to leave a message at the sheriff's office. Her only other choice was to spend the night in the hotel again.

Walking into the hotel, she saw Eliza at the front desk. "Eliza, could I stay here tonight?"

"Goodness sakes, child! What's happened to you?"

Sarah looked around to see if anyone was around. Then she leaned forward and quietly said, "I told Matthew where I was from, and he didn't take it well."

"Not again! Another man who can't face the truth and can't see that it doesn't matter! As long as I live, child, I will not understand men!" Eliza shook her head. "Sarah, I know this doesn't mean much now, but I can tell you that Matthew cares about you, and I am certain it will blow over. It did with Josiah, and believe me, he's much more difficult than Matthew!"

"Thanks, Eliza. That makes me feel a little better, but not much. He is so nonchalant about everything else, I didn't think it would bother him. What a surprise I got." She slowly shook her head from side to side and wiped a tear from the corner of her eye. "Anyway, can I have the room again tonight? I'll figure out what to do tomorrow after I have breakfast with Jenna."

"Of course, dear. Where is your bag?"

"Still over there." Sarah motioned with her head across the street.

"Would you like me to have Samuel go and get it for you?"

"No, I'm fine. I can sleep in my undies, and it won't kill me to wear the same dress two days in a row."

Eliza laughed. "Yes, Sarah, I did notice that I've never seen you wear the same dress twice in all the time you've been coming here!"

Sarah smiled, but found no humor in it. She held out her hand, and Eliza gave her the key. As Sarah walked up the stairs, she turned around and called down, "Please, Eliza, I don't want anyone to disturb me today."

She lay down on the bed without taking her dress off and cried herself to sleep. When she awoke several hours later, she felt better. Not that she had everything in perspective, but she had an innate feeling that everything would be all right. Still, she didn't feel great and had no intention of getting up to socialize, and especially no intention of going back to the saloon.

She pulled her smartphone out of her pocket to look at the time. Shaking her head, she regretted that she couldn't call Jenna right now. There were some things about the old Red Bluff that annoyed the hell out of her. In a fit of anger, she threw the smartphone against the wall. It was in a case, but when it hit, she heard the glass screen shatter. "Damn it!" she said aloud. "Damn it, damn it, damn it!"

Crying about her beloved smartphone gave way to crying about the situation with Matthew. Sarah still couldn't believe the way he had acted. It wasn't anything like the Matthew that she knew—or thought she knew. Although, finding out that someone you might love is from another century *is* a big burden to bear. And hearing it for the first time . . . well, it must have really shocked him. She couldn't blame him. Probably, if she gave him enough time, he would get over it. Probably.

She hoped it wouldn't take too much time. There was no way she could return to her job now. She hated it. Her small annoyances there had become huge irritations, and she wasn't going to deal with it any longer. If her condo didn't sell any time soon, she would rent it out. With the gold coins she received from her tips, she could afford to pay her mortgage and stay here, too.

What if Matthew never got over it? She decided that she wasn't even going to consider that possibility. He would get over it. Soon. Just like Josiah did. And thinking of Josiah, Sarah felt certain that Matthew would talk to Eliza *and* Josiah. She had deliberately told him that Eliza and Josiah had been to the future. At the time, she thought that if he knew someone from his time had gone to her time and survived it, it would make it less of an obstacle. It didn't work at the time. He still reacted badly. But he hoped that after he talked to Eliza and Josiah, he would come to accept her for who she was: a woman from the future, but a woman who cared deeply for him.

Yes, she had finally come to realize the truth of her feelings. Sarah did care deeply for him. Was that love? It was hard to admit, but yes, it was love. She loved Matthew. And her idea of telling him where she was from before it got too serious between them, had been a good idea, but was too late. It was already serious between them. The question was, did Matthew feel that way, too?

CHAPTER NINETEEN

MATTHEW PACED AROUND the room a few minutes after Sarah left, until Zack called, "Matthew! We've got people in the saloon. You coming down or should I take over behind the bar?"

Matthew, still aggravated from his conversation with Sarah, could barely speak. All he could get out was, "You!" Zack must have understood, because Matthew heard the door close behind him.

Matthew exhaled quickly through his nose. That dang woman! Why did she have to surprise him with such information? From the future! Of all the crazy things to happen! Falling for a woman from the future! Just his luck! And the worst part—or maybe the best part—was that he didn't care. Sure, he *was* in a pucker about what she had told him. And although it bothered him, it didn't make him sour on her. Because, did it really matter? He still wasn't sure of the answer to that one, but he *was* sure that he loved her.

He walked out of his bedroom into the living room. Taking another deep breath, he exhaled slowly and opened the door to the hallway. Sarah didn't go into her room—he knew that because while he was in his room, he had heard her walking all the way down the hall. So where did she go? Back to the future? No, probably not. She left her bags here. Matthew suspected she either went to Jenna's house or across the street to the hotel.

He decided that he wouldn't go to her, though. She probably needed time to think about his bad actions, just as he needed time to think about the information she surprised him with. Would she forgive him? He didn't know and had no way of knowing. And although he didn't care that she was from the future, or at least he didn't think he cared, he knew that he did need to speak to Eliza and Josiah about it.

Matthew straightened up, then strode out the door and down the stairs. He walked briskly through the saloon, waved to Zack, and said, "I'll be back. Thanks!" and continued out through the swinging doors.

When he walked into the hotel, Eliza wasn't there. He knocked on the open door leading to their living quarters. "Eliza! It's me, Matthew. Can I talk to you for a minute?"

Eliza came out from the kitchen wiping her hands on a towel. She smiled and nodded at him. "I expected to see you here. Come on in and sit with me."

Matthew walked in and sat across from Eliza. He didn't lean back in his chair—he sat forward, elbows on his knees, wringing his hands.

"Oh, stop that," said Eliza, as she put a hand over his. "Everything will work out if you want it to."

"Do I want it to?" asked Matthew. Then he shook his head and looked down at his hands. "No—I mean, yes, I do. But, Eliza, Sarah talked to me this morning." Matthew looked down at his hands again. It was so foreign to him, he didn't even know how to broach the subject. Yes, he did. Just do it. "Eliza, tell me about the future."

Eliza sat back in her chair and gazed at him. "Sarah told you about it, didn't she?"

"Yes, but I don't understand."

"I admit, it's difficult to understand. It just is. I've been there."

"Oh," said Matthew and pulled back from her as if he could catch it from her. "Then it's true."

"I know Sarah well enough to know that she would not lie to you, son. She told you the truth."

"But how can something like that be?"

"I can tell you honestly that I have no idea. When Sarah and Jenna first started coming here, I noticed some things that didn't make sense to me. So when Jenna told me about the future, it all made more sense. Of course, I insisted that she take me there, because I wanted to see for myself."

"It would scare me. What's it like over there?"

"Indescribable. There are things there that you wouldn't believe could possibly exist. Just the items inside Jenna's house were unbelievable. And outside—what they use instead of wagons or stagecoaches—they take your breath away." She leaned closer to him and whispered, "I rode in a car."

Matthew leaned back and looked at the ceiling. "This is too much for me. I'm not sure I can handle it."

"Of course you can, Matthew! Don't be such a fraidy-cat! You know that Ryan is from there, also, and Rachel, and Granny. Granny is from there! Edward doesn't care."

"Yes, but she's old."

Matthew didn't notice the sound on the stairs, but then Granny burst into the room. "Did I hear someone call me old? You little whippersnapper! I bet I can ride better 'n you, rope better 'n you, shoot better 'n you, and do everything else better 'n you. Anything you can do, I can do better! There! What do you say about that, young fella? You watch who you're callin' old!"

Edward, right behind her, said, "Yeah, Matthew! You watch it!" And then he started laughing.

Eliza laughed, and Matthew had to laugh, too. It was the lightest he had felt since Sarah told him. Yes, he thought, he could handle this. It wasn't a big deal. Look at Edward and Granny. Look at Josiah and Jenna. Edward and Josiah weren't afraid to get involved with someone from the future. He could do this!

Matthew put out his hands in defense. "Okay, okay. You're better 'n me, Granny. I surrender." Then he looked at Eliza. "Okay, I can do this. Do you know where Sarah is?" Matthew stood up. Granny and Edward had disappeared into the other room.

Eliza stood and looked at him. "Yes, she's upstairs, Matthew." She held out a hand to stop him from turning away. "But you can't go up there. She doesn't want to be disturbed."

"Even for me to apologize? Wouldn't she like to hear that?"

"No, Matthew. She needs some time to set with this. You need to leave that girl alone right now. And what *you* need to do is talk to Josiah. But I don't know when he'll be back. He and Jenna went on a picnic today, but he will be back to check on Nick later. Josiah has been the only law in this town for so long, he doesn't know how to act with someone else responsible to take over."

"Okay, Eliza. Thank you. Thank you for your words of advice, and thank you for telling me I should see Josiah. That makes perfect sense to me. I'll check for him later this afternoon."

"You might want to check in with Nick and tell him to have Josiah come see you. That way you won't miss him."

"Good idea, Eliza. Thanks again," said Matthew, as he walked out the door.

CHAPTER TWENTY

MATTHEW FELT BETTER after talking to Eliza, but he couldn't say that he felt good. He wished that Sarah had never told him about being from the future. No, that's not right. He wished that Sarah *wasn't* from the future. That would be the ideal situation. But she was, and he had to decide whether he could handle it or not. He thought he could, and that would be his tentative decision until after he talked to Josiah. Maybe Josiah would give him some information that would change his mind. But with the way that Josiah acted around Jenna, he doubted it. Josiah had never been happier.

After crossing the street, he peeked over the swinging doors of the saloon to see if Zack was okay. He was behind the bar looking busy, and the few people in there had drinks in front of them. Good. Sometimes Zack would sit in the corner with his book and wouldn't even hear anyone call him.

Matthew turned to the right, crossed the street, and walked the short distance to the sheriff's office. As he opened the door and stepped in, he saw Nick sitting at the desk. They hadn't been introduced yet, so Matthew stuck out his hand.

"Hallo, Nick. I'm Matthew. I own the saloon a couple of doors down."

Nick stood up and shook his hand. "Hello, Matthew. Yes, I remember seeing you there the other night. What can I help you with?"

"Could you leave a note for Josiah to come see me when he gets a chance? As soon as he can, really. I know he's on a picnic right now."

"Yeah, he should be in sometime this afternoon to check on me and make sure everything is all right. He's still not used to leaving *his town* in the hands of someone else.

"You're sure it's nothing I can help you with, Matthew?" Nick asked.

Matthew shook his head, slowly blinked his eyes, and looked down. "No, it's about—about the future."

"The future?" asked Nick.

"Yes, it's about Sarah. She told me where she was from, and I'm still trying to get used to it. See, I—oh! You and Sarah . . . ?" Matthew asked, as he looked sheepishly at Nick.

"Me and Sarah? Oh! No! No, Sarah and I are good friends, that's all. I've known her forever. She's like my sister."

"Oh, okay. Well, anyway, Sarah told me, and I'm not sure about it. It bothers me. And I thought if I could talk to Josiah about him and Jenna—well, maybe that would make me feel better."

"I could take you to the future if you'd like. If that would make you feel better. Any of us could."

"No, I don't think that would make me feel any better. I'm not comfortable with that."

"You need to relax, Matthew. It's not like she's a ghost or anything. We're only human, just like you. Sarah's from the *new* Red Bluff, and you're from the old. What's the big deal with that?"

"When you put it that way, it doesn't sound like such a big deal. You're right, Nick. And that does make me feel better. But could you still have Josiah come see me before he goes back home today?"

Nick smiled. "Of course. And Matthew, Sarah's quite a girl. I wouldn't let her go if I were you."

Matthew smiled at him and walked out of the office. As he walked down the street toward the saloon, he kept smiling. What Nick said did make sense. She's just like me. There's nothing *wrong* with her just because she's from the future. Why am I bothered by this? He walked into the saloon thinking what a silly thing to be concerned about. Yes, it was unusual. But wasn't that part of what he loved about Sarah—that she was an unusual girl? This made her more unusual. Matthew was beginning to like that she was from the future. Although he still wanted to talk to Josiah about it.

Back at the saloon, serving drinks, Matthew kept smiling. He could hardly wait to tell Sarah how happy he was that she was from another time. It didn't matter to him. It really didn't matter to him! He loved her. He loved *all* of her—regardless of where she was from. Wait till he saw her tomorrow! He would throw his arms around her and show her how much it did not bother him. Well, maybe he wouldn't exactly do that, but he would tell her.

Several hours later, Josiah showed up. Matthew was glad that Jenna wasn't with him, because although he had finally accepted that Sarah was from another time, he still wanted to ask Josiah some questions, alone.

"Hi, Josiah, thanks for stopping by."

"No problem, Matthew, what can I do for you?"

"Did Nick tell you what I wanted to talk to you about?"

"No, he just said you wanted to see me," said Josiah.

Matthew took a deep breath and glanced around. No one was in hearing distance if he talked quietly. "I want to talk to you about the future. Sarah told me where she's from."

Josiah smiled. "It shocked you, didn't it? Because it sure shocked me when Jenna told me. I didn't think it would work between us, and I pushed her away. I'm glad she didn't go back there and never return."

"I'm afraid I reacted rather badly," said Matthew. "I locked myself in my room and wouldn't talk to her!"

Josiah shook his head. "Not good, Matthew, not good. What did you want to know?"

"Does it matter? I mean, does it matter to you that Jenna is from there?"

"Not at all. Not anymore, anyway. I'm perfectly comfortable with it."

"If you had the choice to do it over, would you rather fall in love with someone else—someone from this time?"

"And lose my Jenna?" asked Josiah, his eyes sparkling. "I wouldn't want to lose my Jenna for all the gold in the world. There is no one like her, and I will love her forever—wherever she's from."

Matthew nodded his head. "Okay, Josiah. Thank you for stopping by. I feel better now."

"What are you going to do?"

"Keep loving her. And hope that she forgives me for being an ass."

"Good luck, Matthew. See you later," said Josiah.

CHAPTER TWENTY-ONE

SEVERAL MORE HOURS passed, and Sarah still lay on the bed going over everything in her head. Not long before, someone had dropped off a tray of food outside her room. She heard someone set the tray down and had waited for the person to walk away. Thank you, Eliza. It was delicious, as usual.

Now, she continued lying on the bed fiddling with her smartphone to see if it would still work with a broken screen. So far, no. And Matthew, damn him! Why had he reacted so badly? He had caught her off guard. His reaction, so cold, so hard, was nothing that she had expected. She knew the information would surprise him, but she didn't think he would pull away like that.

Honestly, she didn't know what to expect. It's not every day that you tell someone that you're from another time. Same place, different time. It was extraordinary. Who could believe it or accept it with a nod and a smile? If someone had told her that, she would have laughed in their face at something so outrageous.

Would Matthew get over it after talking to Eliza and Josiah? Would they soothe his fears and his doubts?

Would Josiah tell him how wonderful it was to be married to a woman from the future? Sarah laughed remembering how Josiah said it was difficult being married to a woman who could vote!

And what of her own feelings? Had she honestly sorted them out? Was she in love with him? She thought so. It felt like it. The way he had reacted earlier in the day had devastated her. She knew she wanted to be with him and only him. But did she want it to be forever? Could she live here without cell phones and without all the modern conveniences that she loved? Then again, how important were those things compared to true love? Could she get past missing those things as easily as Jenna had? She honestly didn't know. Time would tell.

Sarah sat up in bed and stuffed two feather pillows behind her. She felt so confused. Why couldn't love be easy? Why couldn't she have fallen for that jerk, Chad? Oh, no. That would have been horrible. The differences between Matthew and Chad were as great as the century between them. She was grateful that Matthew was nothing like Chad—which was one reason she loved him.

Thinking of love in association with Matthew was beginning to feel easier and easier. Yes, it was the right word to describe how she felt about him. There was no doubt about it now. She wanted to put her shoes on, rush across the street, and throw herself into his arms. But she wouldn't. She still didn't know how he felt after her confession. And how would he feel if she did something so aggressive? Sarah nodded her head when she remembered how he had said the woman should ask him to marry her. So he'd be fine if she threw herself in his arms. They'd both be fine.

But she couldn't do it now. Sarah still needed to gauge

his reaction *after* he talked to Eliza and Josiah. She hoped everything would work out fine, and tomorrow night this time she would be singing in his saloon, and he would be looking at her with the light of love in his eyes. She hoped.

Sarah took off her dress—wrinkled now from lying on the bed all day—and crawled underneath the covers. Although she had slept much of the afternoon, she still felt sleepy. Worrying about how a man felt about you was difficult work! She did think, though, that everything would work out. Eliza and Josiah would certainly relieve his fears. Josiah was so madly in love with Jenna that you could feel it across the room. Would/could/did Matthew love her that much? She would find out soon enough. With that thought, Sarah fell peacefully asleep.

CHAPTER TWENTY-TWO

SARAH WOKE UP, sat up, and stretched. Oh! She hadn't set the alarm on her phone because she broke it. But she could still see the time through the broken screen. Eight-thirty already. She'd be late for breakfast. It took a half hour to ride over to Jenna's, and it would probably take her a half hour to get ready.

Sarah quickly dressed and walked downstairs. Eliza was at the front desk. "Morning, Eliza. Thank you for supper! It was delicious! That was so thoughtful of you, thank you."

"I knew you needed to keep up your strength, dear," said Eliza.

Sarah handed her some money. "Here's for the room and the supper. Did Matthew stop by yesterday?"

"Yes, and he wanted to come up to see you, but I told him you needed some time alone."

"Thank you, Eliza. You're right. I did. Um, what do you think?"

"I think you have nothing to worry about, child. Everything with you and Matthew will turn out just fine. Are you going over there now?"

"No, I wanted to change clothes before I left, but I'm late for breakfast at Jenna's. I need to get Dancer and ride over there right away. I'll see Matthew when I return."

"Good luck then, Sarah. See you later."

"Bye, Eliza," said Sarah, as she hurried out the door and down the street toward the livery stable. She'd lose more time having to saddle Dancer because she hadn't told Ezra that she needed him this morning. When she arrived at the livery a couple of minutes later, she found Dancer already saddled.

"Ezra! How did you know?"

Ezra laughed. "Jenna stopped in yesterday to see Dolly, and she told me. She said it would surprise you."

"Thanks, Ezra!" Sarah climbed onto Dancer and guided him down the street and out of town toward Jenna's ranch.

Sarah figured she was a half hour late for breakfast. She wasn't sure how long Jenna would wait for her, but regardless, she'd run into her on the trail, anyway. It was the quickest way to town from her ranch. As she relaxed into the horse's easy rhythm, she thought about Matthew. She'd enjoy her breakfast with Jenna, but she could hardly wait to get back to Red Bluff and talk to Matthew—get their "first fight" behind them.

She thought about his smile and how good-looking he was. And then she thought about how kind he was. Although she had never considered that important to her, she did now. She loved Matthew's kindness and how well he treated her. Perhaps she hadn't considered it important before because the men she used to be attracted to possessed no kindness at all. It wasn't that they were all mean—they were just all business with no time for thoughtfulness or concern for anyone else. When she was with Carl, he always had his secretary buy her presents and even the cards that he gave to her. And he only remembered because his secretary put it on his calendar.

She couldn't imagine Matthew doing anything like that. He would always remember by himself, and he would always pick out the card or gift for her by himself. Because Matthew was kind. Kindness, she thought, was what defined Matthew. Even taking on Zack was done out of kindness. Sarah thought her heart would burst from the love that she felt for him.

Dancer moved to the left, and Sarah, thinking he was shying away from something, guided him forward. Then she went back to thinking about Matthew. What would it be like living in his apartment with him? Cozy. Loving. She longed to be in his arms right now, kissing him, loving him.

That was one disadvantage of living in the old Red Bluff. There was no phone service. So there was no way she could have canceled breakfast with Jenna. Ah, well. She always enjoyed talking to Jenna. It would be a good morning, and *then* she would go back to Matthew.

Sarah looked around. Wait. She didn't recognize where she was. Glancing behind her, she saw Jenna's ranch in the distance. She had already passed it. That must have been why Dancer veered to the left. Rubbing the horse on the neck, she said, "Sorry, Dancer, I didn't believe you."

As she moved the reins to turn the horse around, a noise from the trees surprised her. Suddenly, a flurry of hooves, feathers, and warpaint. Five Indians, yipping and screaming, surrounded her. Oh, no, she thought. The renegade Indians!

CHAPTER TWENTY-THREE

"Lady," one Indian said with an accent that Sarah didn't recognize, "you in da wrong place at da wrong time!"

She wanted to try to run for it—Dancer was fast—but all their horses pressed so close to her that she couldn't even turn around.

"Let 'er go; let's burn down the ranch like we planned!" said another man.

He said it in plain ol' American English. Sarah looked around at the men. They weren't Indians. They were white men dressed up like Indians. She wasn't sure if this was better or worse. Then she found out.

One man pushed through until his horse was right next to hers. He grabbed her arm hard until she screamed out, "Oww!"

"Shut up, bitch!" he said, and with his other hand he slapped her across the face.

Shocked, she looked at him. "I know you! You're that jerk bigot from the saloon. You're no Indian! Isn't this wicked irony? The bigot dressed up like an Indian!"

"I said shut up!" He slapped her again.

"Damn you, Lucius! Now she knows! Now we're going to have to kill her." The man took the gun from his holster.

Lucius held up his hand. "No, Sanford! Not now. I want to take her first. She's a bitch, but she's beautiful. Let's not waste it." He dismounted, pulled Sarah off her horse, and started dragging her into the trees.

"Not now, idiot! Let's get out of here. You can have her later. We all can. But not here. Let's go back to the shack."

"Damn it! Okay, but I'm first!" He pushed Sarah back toward Dancer and gave her a boost up into the saddle while feeling her butt. Then he took the reins, pulled them over Dancer's head, and climbed onto his own horse.

"He doesn't pony well," said Sarah, as the horses began moving farther away from Jenna's ranch.

"What you say, bitch? Pony?" asked Lucius.

"My horse doesn't pony—oh, you know, lead. He doesn't like to be led."

"I'm sure he'll be fine. Just hold on, bitch."

For the first mile, Dancer was fine, and Sarah thought maybe he had improved since the last time she had tried to pony him. Then, in a narrow spot on the trail, Lucius's horse moved over and touched Dancer, who immediately reared up, pulled away from Lucius, and took off down the trail at a dead run. Sarah thought if it was any other time, she would do an emergency dismount. When Dancer realized he had lost his rider, he would stop. But right now, it was a bigger emergency getting away from the outlaw hoodlums. If Dancer didn't trip on the reins hanging down, he could easily outrun the other horses. Dancer was a thoroughbred retired from the track.

What she didn't expect was—a rope. One minute she was leaning forward with the wind blowing in her face hoping to escape the crazies, and the next minute she felt the rope tighten across her chest and pull her backward. She landed with a hard thud on her back that knocked the wind out of her. Then she lay there trying to catch her breath.

As Sarah expected, Dancer stopped when he felt an empty saddle. Relieved of his rider, he grazed on some grass he had found on the side of the trail.

Lucius jerked on the rope and said, "Get up, bitch." When Sarah didn't move, he stepped over and kicked her in the side. "That's what you get for tryin' to escape!"

Sarah coughed and sat up painfully. "I wasn't trying to escape—I told you the horse didn't lead well. I didn't even have the reins, you idiot!" She knew she shouldn't goad him, but she couldn't help it.

"Come 'ere, you big mouth bitch!"

Lucius grabbed her and put his mouth to hers, forcing his tongue between her lips. She pushed him away and spat in his face. He swung his arm and hit her hard in the face, knocking her backward.

"Lucius! Leave her alone or there won't be anything left for the rest of us. Stop beating on her! Boost her up behind me," said Sanford.

"Her hoss is right over there," Lucius said and pointed to the horse who had wandered down the road.

"Leave him. The horse won't lead, and it will just cause more trouble," said Sanford.

"Then I'll shoot him," said Lucius who pulled out his gun and cocked it.

"Lucius, no! Damn it! Leave the damn horse and get

the girl up behind me. We don't need to be drawing anyone's attention with a gunshot. We've got the woman, now let's go someplace safe where we can use her. Come on!"

Lucius, grumbling, helped Sarah up behind Sanford, giving her butt another squeeze as he boosted her up. Then he returned to his own horse and mounted up.

Sarah hurt all over. Her face hurt from the slap, her butt and back hurt from the fall, and her side hurt where Lucius had kicked her. Luckily, the horses moved slowly enough that Sarah didn't have to hang on to Sanford. All she could think about was that a few minutes ago she was imagining what it would be like to make love to Matthew, and now unless a miracle occurred, she was about to get gang-banged by these nineteenth-century hoodlums. And then probably shot dead.

CHAPTER TWENTY-FOUR

MATTHEW HADN'T SLEPT well. He had tossed and turned all night long with thoughts of his "reunion" with Sarah. He had overcome his apprehension of Sarah coming from the future. And he was ready to embrace her into his life forever. If that was what she wanted, too. And he thought she did. He'd find out soon enough.

Matthew was halfway down the flight of stairs when he thought of something and stopped. Turning around, he climbed two stairs at a time back to the top. He walked down to Sarah's room and knocked on the door. Although he knew she had spent the night at the hotel, he didn't want to interrupt her accidentally in case she had come back up here without his knowledge.

Opening the door, he stepped in and inhaled the scent of her. Maybe it was his imagination, but the room smelled like her already, and she hadn't even slept there yet. Then he saw the three bags that she had left there. He leaned down and sniffed one. Sure enough, it smelled just like the lovely Sarah. As he stood up straight, he knitted his brows. Three bags full of clothes. Wherever was she going to put it all? He knew exactly where, and he would take care of it himself later. Knowing that last time Sarah had breakfast with Jenna, she hadn't returned until late afternoon, he had plenty of time.

Matthew closed Sarah's door and walked downstairs. After fixing himself eggs for breakfast, he began restocking the bar area. Normally, he did that every day, but with everything on his mind lately, it had been forgotten.

Everything on his mind. Who was he kidding? He knew exactly what had been on his mind—what was completely consuming his thoughts—and that was Sarah. His Sarah. At least he hoped she would be his soon. There was nothing more that he wanted in this whole world than to have that woman forevermore. He hoped that she felt the same way.

But she was from the future! Although he had lost his apprehension, he still wondered about the differences between them. What did women from the future think about? Then Jenna came to mind. It wasn't just that she was happily married to Josiah. There wasn't anything he could think of that made her different from any other woman in Red Bluff. Except maybe her speech. Occasionally, Jenna—and Sarah did it, too—would say something that made no sense to him at all. Otherwise, Jenna —and Sarah—seemed like ordinary women. They both may be unusual, but nothing would make anyone think they were from a time a century in the future.

Matthew, lost in his thoughts about Sarah, heard Zack come down the stairs and said, "Mornin', Zack."

"Mornin', Matthew. You're bright and cheery this morning." Zack sat down at the bar.

"Sarah should be coming back soon."

"She was upset yesterday when she left. You sure she's coming back?"

Matthew tilted his head and said, "Well, her bags are here, so she has to return. Besides that, she and I need to talk, and I think she knows that. I did something terrible to her, Zack, and I need to apologize."

Zack sat up straight and stiffened his shoulders. "You didn't hurt her, did you?"

Matthew smiled at Zack's defense of Sarah. He put his arms out and motioned down. "Calm down, Zack. I didn't do anything to her like that. I said something to her that might have hurt her, and then I locked myself in the bedroom and refused to talk to her."

"Oh, yeah, I walked in right after that."

Matthew nodded. "Yes, she was upset. But I'm going to make it up to her, and I won't ever do that again. I—I love her."

Zack grinned. "You do? Are you going to marry her? Will she stay with us here then, and not go back to her other job?"

"Easy, boy, easy. One thing at a time. I don't know what will happen."

Zack's grin faded. "What if she won't forgive you? What if she's still mad at you from what you did yesterday?"

"I think everything will be fine, Zack. She and I will talk today and work everything out. At least I hope so."

"I hope so, too, Matthew. I really like Sarah."

"I'm confident that we can work everything out. That's why I'm bright and cheery. Because I'm *sure* we can work everything out."

CHAPTER TWENTY-FIVE

MATTHEW PUTTERED AROUND the saloon until after ten o'clock. Then he walked down the street to see Ryan at the general store. Opening the door, he saw Ryan at the counter giving a rancher's wife change. She put the money in her purse and hurried out with her wrapped package in her arms.

"Hallo, Ryan!" said Matthew.

"Hey, Matthew. How's that composting toilet working out for you?"

"No complaints. I was wondering if you had anything like a ready-made chest of drawers?"

"Nothing out here. Let me check in the back." Ryan disappeared into the back room. "No, sorry, nothing there, either."

"Can you get me the materials to build one, then?"

"That I can do!" said Ryan. "I already have some stuff, but not all of it. Do you want to take what I have or wait until I get it all?"

"I'll wait, thank you." Matthew turned to go.

"Oh, wait, Matthew. How big would you like it?"

"About this high and this wide," Matthew held his

hand five feet off the ground and then spread out his arms. "It's for Sarah."

Ryan laughed. "Matthew, if it's for Sarah, that's not going to be big enough! I better get you enough material for two!"

Matthew smiled at him. "I forgot that you know Sarah from, um, before. I think I'll build just the one for now, and we'll see. Thanks, Ryan!"

Matthew stepped outside and inhaled deeply, feeling satisfied with himself. He had taken another step to make Sarah more comfortable living upstairs from the saloon. Movement to his left caught his attention. It was Jenna on her horse, Magic, headed toward the livery.

"Hallo, Jenna! You two must have had a quick breakfast today."

"She's not with you, Matthew? I thought that's why she didn't show up. I waited an hour, and when she didn't show, I came back into town. Josiah doesn't want me to stay there by myself with those renegade—" She looked at Matthew and her eyes got wide. "Oh, no. She must be somewhere in town."

Matthew wanted to cry, but instead he stayed perfectly calm. "Jenna, you check the livery and see if she took her horse—that will tell us if she's still in town. I'll go see Josiah." Matthew turned around and ran to the sheriff's office. Bursting in, he said, "Josiah! Nick! It's Sarah! I think the renegades have her! What are we going to do?"

"Don't have a conniption fit, Matthew," said Josiah. "She went to meet Jenna for—"

Matthew interrupted him. "No! Jenna just got to town and said that Sarah never showed up. She went to the livery to see if her horse is gone. What are we going to do?"

Josiah pulled his pocket watch out of his pocket. "It's nearly half past ten. She was supposed to meet Jenna at nine. That means they could have an hour and a half head start on us. We need to move now. Matthew, if you and Zack want to go, get your horses quickly and meet us back here."

Matthew ran down the street and into the bar. "Zack! Zack! Get our guns! Sarah's missing! I'll be right back with the horses!" he shouted. Then he ran around the corner to the livery. Ezra had two horses saddled and ready for him.

"Matthew, Jenna told me, and I thought you and Zack would want to go. Here, these two are fast! She already took Josiah's and Nick's horses. Good luck!" said Ezra.

"Thanks, Ezra!"

Matthew jumped into the saddle and rode back to the saloon. Zack was waiting outside with his gun belt strapped on and holding a rifle and a second gun belt. As Matthew approached, Zack ran out to him, handed him the second gun belt and rifle, and climbed onto the other horse. Matthew could just see Nick and Josiah heading out of town. He quickly put the gun belt on and slid the rifle into the scabbard. Then, he and Zack raced after them.

CHAPTER TWENTY-SIX

SARAH FELT SHAKEN. The horses had been trotting for well over an hour. She was already sore from the fall and the kick, and the rough ride made it worse. Dancer had such a smooth trot—she wished she were on him instead of riding double on this horse. That thought almost made her laugh aloud. Here she was, kidnapped by these thugs, and what did she think about? How smooth Dancer's trot was! Still, she was sore.

She sighed and said, "How much farther until we get where we're going?"

Sanford answered by giving her an elbow to her ribs. It was so unexpected that it almost made her tumble off the horse. So she instinctively grabbed Sanford for balance—which made him elbow her again. She released him and shook her head. She was in a bad spot. And there wasn't anything she could do about it.

Sanford spoke over his shoulder, but loud enough for the others to hear. "You've been so much damn trouble, bitch, that you can expect we will make good use of you before we blow your brains out. And I'm not talking about cooking us supper!" Sanford and the others laughed.

Sarah felt devastated. Would they rescue her in time? Would they rescue her at all? How long, she wondered, would it take for them to realize she was missing? The first question would be how long would Jenna wait for her? Since she was normally on time, she didn't think Jenna would wait more than an hour. Would Dancer have wandered back to the ranch by then? If he had, Jenna would know immediately. They had been riding together long enough to know that if Sarah lost her seat, Dancer would stand around and wait for her to remount.

But after Dancer took off when Lucius tried to pony him, they had gotten even farther from the ranch. With so much grass on the sides of the road, Dancer wouldn't make it back to the ranch anytime soon. And if he did manage to find his way back there, Jenna would have already left.

Once Jenna got to town, she would probably assume that Sarah was with Matthew and wouldn't want to disturb her. That left Matthew. How long would it take for him to realize she was missing? It was possible that he would think that she was mad at him. And if Eliza had told him that Sarah was having breakfast with Jenna, then Matthew might think she wouldn't return until late afternoon like the last time when she was late.

The more she thought about it, the more she realized that she was screwed. Figuratively now with no hope for a rescue, and literally later when the hoodlums had their way with her. Sarah had imagined that Matthew would be slow and gentle when they made love. These guys would be anything but slow and gentle. She felt scared.

She knew that to survive in disastrous situations, one had to maintain hope. But right then she felt helpless and hopeless. No one even knew she was missing! How would they know to come rescue her? When Jenna and Josiah went back to the ranch in the late afternoon, they would certainly notice Dancer then. But by that time, the deed would be done, and she would be dead.

They turned their horses off the main road and onto a widened path through the trees. Sanford interrupted her thoughts.

"We're almost there, now, bitch. And am I ever ready for you!" He reached back, grabbed her hand roughly, and placed it on his crotch. He held it there momentarily, and she felt his hardness before she could pull her hand away.

"Don't get any ideas, Sanford! She's mine first! I found her!"

"Lucius, you may have a fight on your hands. I like the feel of her next to me. I want her first. She's mine."

"Damn it, Sanford! I called it!" Lucius reined his horse over to Sanford and tried to take a swing at him.

Sanford pushed him away. "Idiot! Not now! We'll settle this when we get there. Leave me alone! We're almost there." Then to Sarah, he said, "Aren't you the popular one!"

Sarah wondered if they'd bury her in the old Red Bluff or the new Red Bluff.

CHAPTER TWENTY-SEVEN

THE HORSES WERE fast, thought Matthew. He and Zack had caught up with Josiah and Nick with no trouble at all. Matthew's horse was a little too much horse for him —Matthew wasn't a cowboy, had never considered himself a cowboy. But the horse would be fine for what Matthew needed of him, and Matthew was certain he could handle him. After all, Sarah needed him to.

Sarah. Oh, Sarah. How long had the renegades had her? What would they do to her? Was she even still alive? Matthew chastised himself. If he had reacted better to Sarah telling him where she was from, then maybe this never would have happened. No, that's not true. She would have gone to breakfast with Jenna regardless.

Matthew could see that it was exactly this that separated Jenna and Sarah from the other women in Red Bluff. No other women in town would risk running into the renegades. But Sarah and Jenna acted like nothing could happen to them. Like they were bulletproof. Thinking about the head start the renegades had, Matthew hoped that Sarah *was* bulletproof.

Matthew felt the rifle in the scabbard that hung off the

saddle. He had never been comfortable with a pistol—but when he started west from Missouri, everyone said he had to have one. His rifle, though, he could handle. On his trip cross-country with Catherin, he had been forced to learn how to shoot effectively, or else they would have gone hungry or been dependent on others for their meals. He learned and had become a good shot.

Josiah and Nick had slowed their horses. Oh, here was Josiah's ranch. At a fast gallop, they had covered the distance quickly. Josiah rode his horse into the barn and back out again.

"Josiah," Zack said, "only one horse has walked in here."

"You're right, Zack, just Jenna's. No sign of Sarah's horse at all. I didn't know you could track!"

"My dad taught me before he, you know, died."

"But your dad wasn't Indian."

"His best friend, my uncle—you know, my mother's brother—taught him all about tracking. I learned some, I'm not very good."

"You're better 'n anybody here. Ride up front, Zack," said Josiah. "Stop us if you see anything."

They hadn't gone far when they noticed Sarah's horse nibbling on some grass at the side of the road. The men stopped, and Josiah dismounted.

"Look, the reins are hanging on the ground. I don't think that he threw Sarah. But we can't be sure. Let's go a little farther."

"Should we bring her horse for when we find her?" asked Matthew.

"No, he'll slow us down. Sarah can ride double with one of us. Let's go," said Josiah.

A minute later, Zack held up his hand and reined in

his horse. He jumped off the horse and knelt on the ground. Josiah and Nick both got off to see what Zack was looking at.

Zack stood up. "Six horses. One of them was probably Sarah's, so we can guess five men. And look at this," he pointed to the hoof marks in the dirt. "Shoes. Indian ponies don't wear shoes. I told you they weren't Indians."

Josiah shook his head. "If these are troublemaking cowboys, Sarah could be in even more danger." He looked up at Matthew. "I'm sorry, Matthew." Josiah and the other two men mounted their horses. "Let's go. We might not have much time. And since we don't know how far, we better slow down, at least for a while. The horses need a break."

"If you look up ahead," Zack said, as he pointed down the road, "it looks like they're trotting, not running. If they're not too far in front of us, we should catch up soon, depending on how much of a head start they had."

The four men raced down the road at an easy canter, with Zack in the lead. Matthew's horse was fast enough that he was right with the other men. But way too much time had passed for Matthew's liking. Where was Sarah? How far ahead could they be? Would they be in time? Matthew's head was swimming with bad possibilities. He told himself to focus on only good outcomes. Sarah being fine. Sarah being rescued. Sarah in his arms.

"Stop," said Zack, as he held up his hand again, then pointed to the side of the trail. "Look, they've turned off here. I think I know where they're going. My father and I used to stay at a little cabin down this trail."

"Great work, Zack! Come on! Let's go rescue Sarah!" said Matthew, as he urged his horse forward.

"Wait," said Josiah. "How far down this trail is it,

Zack?"

"Not far. Ten minutes at a walk. But I know a shortcut. I doubt if they took it—it was overgrown back when we used to ride here."

"We need to surprise them. Zack, if we run for a couple of minutes, would they be close enough to hear us coming?" asked Josiah.

"If they're already at the cabin, then no, not if you stop soon enough. You should stop at the shortcut. I'll show you where it is and then circle behind them."

"Let's go," said Josiah.

They galloped down the road until Zack held up his hand to stop. "The horses went straight. They don't know about the shortcut!" said Zack. "You need to walk the horses in from here. And—"

"Wait, Zack. Show us the layout of the cabin," said Nick.

Zack jumped off his horse, found a sharp stick, and drew a box in the dirt to show the cabin. "There are no windows on the sides of the cabin. The windows are all in the front, so they can't see you coming if you approach on the side. There is an old hitching post in front of the cabin, but last time I was there, it was falling down. In the back, there is a corral. A heavy growth of trees surrounds the cabin on three sides. I'll be coming in from this side."

"Great. Thanks, Zack," said Nick.

"Zack, make sure your gun is loaded," said Josiah. "And where's the shortcut?"

Zack pointed into a spot between two thick bushes. No one could tell there was a trail there without already knowing about it, thought Matthew. How lucky that Zack was with us.

105

"Good luck, Zack!" said Josiah.

"Good luck. Matthew, we'll get her. Don't worry." Zack squeezed Matthew's arm and then guided his horse between the two bushes.

CHAPTER TWENTY-EIGHT

SARAH COULD SEE the cabin up ahead. They'd be there in less than five minutes. She closed her eyes tight to pretend that this wasn't happening. But when she opened them again, everything was the same, and they were that much closer to the cabin—and her fate. Tears formed at the corners of Sarah's eyes and silently rolled down her cheeks. There was no sign of rescue. Maybe living in the old west wasn't all that it was cracked up to be.

Sanford reined in his horse and said, "Get off, bitch. I'm almost ready for you now. And don't even think of running off, or I swear I'll shoot you down." Then to the others, he said, "Boys, take the horses to the back."

Sarah slid off the horse, and Sanford swung his leg over and stood next to her. Lucius came up from behind and tackled him. Sarah backed away slowly toward the trees to the right of the cabin. As Lucius was trying to kick him, Sanford grabbed his foot and pulled him down. "Damn it, Lucius, wait a minute." Sanford hurried to his feet, took two steps toward Sarah, and tackled her. With Sanford's added weight, Sarah hit the ground hard. "Stay there, bitch, if you know what's good for you."

Sanford stood up quickly and immediately lunged at Lucius. Sarah watched from the ground like an uninvolved observer. She didn't care who won. And the fight over her was just delaying the inevitable. Thoughts of Matthew crossed her mind, and she felt sad that everything that she had hoped for them would never happen now. Why didn't she realize her feelings before? Then maybe none of this would have happened. Why did she have to keep fighting it? She knew the answer to that one: she was afraid—afraid of getting involved with a nice man. Now it was too late for regrets and too late for love.

Sanford and Lucius were still fighting a few feet away from her. Although Sanford was bigger, Lucius was faster and able to get away from some of the bigger man's punches. Then Sanford connected a hard punch to Lucius's face, and Lucius fell down. Sanford kicked him a couple of times in the side and said, "That's for jumping me from behind, you idiot!"

After one final kick, Sanford walked toward Sarah. He unbuckled his gun belt and put it gently on the ground. Then he unbuttoned the top button of his pants, put out his arms, gave out a "hiyiiiii," and flew toward Sarah. He landed on her with a hard thump, and her head hit the ground.

"Now for the good part, lady!" Sanford tried to kiss her but she moved her head to avoid him. Holding her down with one arm and with the other pulling her skirt and petticoat up, he ripped her panties off. Then he reached down to undo his own pants. Sarah closed her eyes, let the tears fall, and braced herself for the worst possible thing that she could ever imagine.

CHAPTER TWENTY-NINE

MATTHEW WANTED TO cry. He felt so skeery at what they would find at the cabin that he could barely hold the reins. Josiah and Nick rode in front of him, and he felt grateful for that. He didn't want them to see the moisture in his eyes. Why did he hesitate when Sarah told him where she was from? What difference did that make to love? Love was love no matter what. He had always believed that, and yet he held back. Whatever happened here, today, he would always regret that. It may have cost him his Sarah.

Josiah and Nick slowed their horses in front of him. "I can see the cabin. Let's leave the horses here and walk the rest of the way in. Matthew, make sure your pistol and your rifle are loaded. Nick, you and Matthew stay on that side of the trail, and I'll stay on this side. Keep to the trees so they can't see us approaching. I know there's no windows on the side, but those old cabins often have spaces between the logs. Stay out of sight! Let's go."

Matthew followed Nick through the heavy growth of trees. His rifle felt heavy in his hands, and the gun belt unfamiliar. Their steps crunching and their arms pushing aside branches sounded so loud in his ears, he wondered if they could hear it in the cabin. Closer and closer and Matthew started feeling sick to his stomach. He didn't know why he felt that way. Was it because what they were doing was so foreign to him? Or because of what he might find once they got there? If anything had happened to Sarah, he didn't know what he'd do.

Matthew had been looking down as he walked behind Nick, trying not to step on anything that made noise. Now he heard a voice, soft but distinct. He looked up and saw a man on top of Sarah on the ground. The man had lifted himself up and was looking forward. Matthew followed his gaze and saw Zack standing there with a gun pointed at the man.

"I said, get off her now," said Zack.

The man looked behind him, and Matthew noticed the gun belt on the ground close by. He wasn't sure if Zack had noticed it. Lifting the rifle, he aimed above the man's head. He knew he was nervous, and he didn't want to shoot Sarah accidentally.

Nick pushed the rifle down and said, "I'll take care of it, Matthew." Then he stepped out into the open with his gun drawn. "Mister, if you reach for that gun belt, you're a dead man. Get off the lady, stand up, and put your hands behind your back." Nick walked toward the man, who had slowly stood up. At the back of Nick's belt, Matthew saw a little pouch. Nick reached back and took a pair of handcuffs from the pouch. When he reached the man, who was now standing, he said, "Hands behind you! Now!" Then with one hand, Nick put the handcuffs on him. Matthew noticed the man's pants were undone.

Zack was helping Sarah up, and she was hugging him. Matthew could finally feel the ground beneath his shaky legs, and he ran over to Sarah and wrapped his arms around her.

"Oh, Matthew, you rescued me! You rescued me! Thank you! Thanks, Zack! You were awesome! Oh, Matthew." Sarah broke down in tears, and Matthew stroked her back.

Josiah, gun out and approaching the other side of the cabin, called out, "Come on, Nick!"

Nick said, "Zack, keep your gun on this jerk!" Then Nick turned and ran after Josiah.

From behind the cabin, Matthew heard someone shout, "Lady! I'll be back for my turn! You just wait! Ha, ha!" Then two gunshots went off, and Matthew heard the sound of galloping horses as the outlaws skedaddled.

Those words, carried through the still afternoon air, sent a chill down Matthew's back. And even worse, he knew that Sarah had heard them, too.

Sarah clung to him, weeping so hard that she couldn't speak. When Nick and Josiah ran over to them, they took control of the handcuffed man. Zack put his gun away and put his arms around the back of Sarah, so she could feel surrounded with love. Matthew knew that Zack had really liked Sarah even before she defended him at the saloon.

"Sarah, are you, are you, ah, okay?" asked Josiah.

Sarah sniffled, tried to catch her breath, and then squeaked out, "Yes, Josiah, you got here in time. Thank you. And thank you, Nick. Thanks to all of you for rescuing me." With that she burst into wracking sobs, and it took both Matthew *and* Zack to comfort her.

Josiah walked over and put his arms around the three of them, with his head touching Sarah's. "It's okay, Sarah, you're safe now. You're safe now," said Josiah.

"I'll go get the horses," said Nick.

A few minutes later, Nick brought the four horses over. Josiah broke away from the embrace.

"Thanks, Nick. Would you mind checking the corral to see if they left a horse there?"

Nick jogged over to the corral, and a minute later returned leading a horse. "This will make it easier," he said.

Nick helped the handcuffed man onto the horse; Josiah mounted his horse and held the other horse's reins in his hand. Nick looked at Matthew, Zack, and Sarah and said, "Matthew, would you like Sarah to ride double with me?"

Matthew thought how kind of Nick to offer—he had noticed that Matthew wasn't comfortable on the horse and probably would be less comfortable with Sarah on the back.

"Yes, Nick, thank you for offering," said Matthew.

Zack pulled away from Sarah, but she clung to Matthew. He tried to unwrap her arms from around his neck, but she cried harder and wouldn't let go.

"Come on, Sarah," Matthew said softly while stroking her back. "You're safe now. We're going home. Come on, let go and we'll go home. I'll keep you safe."

Saying that made Matthew wince because he hadn't kept her safe thus far. But he had to ignore his own feelings of inadequacy now and take care of Sarah. He continued stroking her back and whispering comforting words to her. Zack and Nick had gotten on their horses.

"Come on, Sarah. You're okay. Let's go home now," said Matthew.

Slowly, so slowly that Matthew could barely tell a difference, Sarah pulled away from him. Tears streaked her beautiful face, and he now noticed some dark marks on her face. He wasn't sure if it was dirt or if those men had hit her. He feared it was the latter.

When she had stepped away from him, he took her arm and gently helped her up onto Nick's horse. Then he mounted his own. As they walked down the trail with Josiah and the handcuffed man in front, Matthew kept his horse next to Nick's and held Sarah's hand as they rode back toward Red Bluff.

CHAPTER THIRTY

SARAH FELT SORE all over, but they walked the horses, so it wasn't so bad. Considering how everything turned out, she realized how lucky she was. It could have been much, much worse. She could have been dead. Raped and dead.

She couldn't look at Sanford after what he had done to her—and what he had almost done. Although he was now in handcuffs, the sight of him so close still upset her. So she had one arm around Nick to hold on, and she rested her head against his back. That way, she could look at Matthew. If she kept her head filled with the sight of Matthew, all the bad things that had happened to her might float away.

Sarah could see that Matthew was having trouble with his horse. The horse wanted to get home, and Matthew had to keep holding it back so he could stay even with her to hold her hand. The horse kept throwing its head, and Matthew didn't know what to do about it. She watched him in silence, as he struggled unwilling to give up.

Although she had a smile on her face, it was a sad

smile. Right now, she felt broken inside. Thoroughly broken. Things like this didn't happen in her Red Bluff. How could she ever feel safe here again? She knew she couldn't—as long as *he* was loose. They had caught Sanford as he was trying to rape her, but Lucius, the one she felt was even more dangerous, was still out there. He said he'd be back. And she believed him. Oh, yes, she believed him.

Finally, they came to Sarah's horse, who was grazing on some grass across from Jenna and Josiah's ranch. "Sarah. There's your horse. We can lead him back for you."

Sarah exhaled and tried to build up enough energy so she could speak. "No, Josiah. He doesn't lead well. I'll ride him. It's okay. I'll be okay." She said it but didn't feel it. No, she would not be okay. She would never be okay again.

Matthew jumped off his horse and helped her down, while Zack got off his horse, caught Dancer, and walked him over to Sarah. Matthew helped her into the saddle. "Are you sure about this, Sarah?" he asked.

She nodded her head. "Yes, Matthew, I'll be fine." No she wouldn't. She knew that.

Matthew and Zack mounted up again, and the five riders headed toward Red Bluff.

Dancer liked moving right along, and Sarah soon found herself with Matthew, in front of Josiah and Sanford. Sanford whistled and said, "She is such a beautiful woman. If that youngster had waited five more minutes, I would have had my fill of her."

Matthew turned in the saddle and said, "Shut pan!"

"Yeah, all the boys were going to take her, but I had first. I was going to—" said Sanford.

115

"Shut up! Shut up or I'll shoot you down!" screamed Matthew.

"Another word out of you, and you'll be walking, not riding," said Josiah. "Or maybe, if I feel like it, I'll drag you all the way back to Red Bluff."

But he had said enough. Tears ran freely down Sarah's face, and she was racked with sobs. Her body shook so violently, she began having trouble controlling Dancer.

Matthew looked behind him with narrowed eyes and said, "Damn you!"

Sanford just laughed. When Josiah looked at him, Sanford stopped laughing. As time went on, Sarah's sobs subsided. But tears still fell down her cheeks. She couldn't stop crying. She wasn't sure if she could ever stop crying.

When they passed the Red Bluff sign at the edge of town, Matthew said, "Sarah, I'll get the wood stove in your room going for you—it'll make you feel all warm and cozy. And I'll bring you a glass of sarsaparilla. That will make you feel better."

Sarah shook her head, but didn't look at him, and didn't say a word.

"You don't want sarsaparilla or you don't want the fire? I'll do whatever you like to make you feel comfortable, to make you feel safe," said Matthew.

"No," said Sarah.

"No?" asked Matthew.

"I'm going home, Matthew. I can't feel safe here. Not now. Not ever again. I want to go home where I'll feel safe."

"You mean back to Eliza's hotel?"

"No, Matthew. My home. My real home. You know." She turned to face him, and her eyes lit up momentarily.

"Come with me!"

"No, Sarah, I can't do that." Matthew looked away, unable to look at her.

"Don't worry, it's okay, Matthew," said Sarah. "Josiah's been there! You'll be fine. Please come home with me."

"No, Sarah, I'm sorry, I can't." Matthew now turned toward her. "But you can come to the saloon. I'll take good care of you. You know I will."

"Matthew, I need to go home."

They were ahead of the group and were now in front of the sheriff's office. As Josiah and Sanford, followed by Nick and Zack, arrived, Sarah turned Dancer back the way they had come.

"Sarah, where are you going?" asked Josiah.

"I'm going home, Josiah. Where I'll feel safe."

"If I need you to testify—"

"You know how to find me, Josiah," said Sarah, as she motioned Dancer forward. Then she turned back for one brief second, looked at Matthew, and said, "Matthew, are you sure—?"

Matthew shook his head and looked away. "I love you, Sarah. I'm sorry."

Without looking back over her shoulder, Sarah said, "I love you, too, Matthew."

CHAPTER THIRTY-ONE

ZACK, SEEING WHAT was going on, said, "Matthew, go with her! I can watch the saloon. Go with Sarah!"

Matthew shook his head as the other riders got off their horses. Then he turned toward the direction that Sarah had gone and watched until she was out of sight. He rubbed the moisture out of his eyes, dismounted, and followed the men into the sheriff's office.

Josiah sat at his desk with pencil and paper in front of him. Nick stood next to the man in handcuffs and kept one hand wrapped around the man's arm. Zack stood behind Josiah, watching. Matthew felt so confused, he barely knew what was going on.

"What is your name?" asked Josiah.

"Sanford," the man said.

"Sanford, what?" asked Josiah.

"Just Sanford."

Josiah exhaled slowly, closed his eyes, and slowly shook his head. Then he dropped the pencil on the desk.

"Nick, take that piece of garbage to the cell."

Nick led the man out, and surprisingly, Josiah followed. So, Zack and Matthew followed, too.

When Nick started to put him in the first cell, Josiah said, "No, the lock is broken on that cell. Put him in the middle one, next to Rawlins."

Nick surreptitiously looked at Josiah, but didn't say anything. Rawlins, in the third cell, was still asleep from the previous night's drunk. Josiah walked into the open cell with Rawlins, as Nick locked up Sanford.

"Rawlins! You didn't take the keys to bed with you again, did you?" asked Josiah, as he gave the sleeping man a shove.

"Huh? What? Huh?" asked Rawlins.

Josiah briefly put his hands on the man's pockets, and satisfied, walked out of the cell. "You're okay, Rawlins, go back to sleep."

"Huh? Yeah," said Rawlins, and a moment later he was once again snoring.

"Why isn't his cell locked?" asked Sanford.

"Not that it's any of your business, but he's the damn deputy!" said Josiah in an angry voice.

"A drunk as the deputy? Ha, ha! That's perfect!"

"Why doesn't Rawlins sleep in the cell with the broken lock?" asked Nick.

"Because he likes that one better, the damn drunk. When he wakes up, make the change, and put Sanford in the cell that Rawlins is in. Keep 'em separate."

"I think I'd be more comfortable in this cell," said Sanford.

"Man, you're as comfortable as you're going to be until you hang."

"Hang? For what? That youngling stopped me before I did anything to the bitch. So I did nothing wrong— nothing to hang for." He smiled a cocky smile.

"Last time I checked, kidnapping was still against the

119

law, Sanford."

"Kidnapping? Are you kidding? That strumpet came with us willingly. She wanted it from all of us. She could hardly wait."

Matthew was seething. He pushed past Josiah, and Nick caught him before he got to the cell.

"Easy, Matthew. Why don't you and Zack get out of here? Josiah and I will be out in a minute. Go, Matthew. You don't need to be here."

Matthew, before walking back, looked back at Sanford and said, "I oughta kill you for what you said. And make you suffer for what you did."

"Matthew, out!" said Josiah. "The man's in jail, and I will deal with it from here. He'll be dealt with after a fair trial."

"He doesn't deserve a fair trial!" said Matthew. "Look what he did to Sarah!"

"Come on, Matthew, let's go," said Zack, as he took Matthew's arm and led him away from the jail cells and outside.

"Take it easy, Matthew. It's going to be all right," said Zack.

"How can it be all right after what they did to Sarah?"

"Don't worry, Matthew. Josiah will take care of it."

Before Matthew had a chance to dispute, Nick and Josiah walked outside. Josiah walked away from the building and motioned the rest of the men to follow.

"Matthew, I know you're upset. But listen to me. I have a plan."

"The only plan I want to hear is where you hang that guy. As soon as possible," said Matthew.

Josiah looked at Matthew. "No, Matthew, that's not my plan. My plan is to let him go."

"Let him go? What? You have to hang him! Why would you let him go? Sarah left because she can't feel safe here. Once he's dead, maybe she'll come back."

"No, Matthew, she won't come back. You heard what that outlaw said as he rode away, didn't you? He said he'd be back to get her. Sarah would never feel safe as long as *he* is loose. We need to catch the rest of the gang, and I have a plan to do that."

Matthew reluctantly nodded his head. "You're right. With that outlaw loose, she couldn't feel safe here. I agree with you. Okay, I'm listening."

After he checked that no one was close enough to hear them, Josiah had the other three men huddle around him, and he whispered his plan to them.

"Yeah, but Rawlins?" asked Matthew. "You can't trust him."

"I think he can do it," said Josiah. "And if not, we can make it look like he did it."

Nick nodded his head and smiled. "I suspected something like this when you said that cell on the end had the lock broken. That's why I didn't say anything. I had checked all the locks when I first started filling in with you, and I knew they all worked fine."

Josiah winked at Nick and smiled. Matthew didn't smile—he couldn't with the way he felt—but he thought the plan had a chance to work. And he knew that it was his only chance to get his Sarah back. He noticed that Zack smiled because he appreciated the confidence that had been placed in him.

121

CHAPTER THIRTY-TWO

IT WAS GOOD that Dancer knew the way home, thought Sarah, because she was crying so hard that she could barely see the trail. She felt like her whole world was falling apart. She had finally figured out that she was in love with Matthew, and now, because of what had happened, she was torn apart from him.

Sarah didn't blame him for not wanting to come with her to her time. Although it made her feel bad, she mostly understood. That was a big leap into the unknown, and she knew Matthew well enough to know that he wasn't a "leaper." Her past men would have done it without question—even if there was considerable danger. But instead of feeling upset by Matthew's lack of risk taking, she felt comforted by it. He was much more stable, more solid, than any other guy she had ever been with—or wanted to be with.

That made her cry even harder, because now he was gone from her, probably for good. She could never return to the old Red Bluff while Lucius was on the loose. And how could they ever catch him? No, her singing days were over, and her budding romance with Matthew was over.

Dancer walked out of the cave and into Sarah's own time. It would have made Sarah's crying increase again, but she felt all cried out. Now she had to get practical. She would take the condo off the market and cancel the rest of her vacation. Either she would find a new job that excited her, or she would learn to love her old one again. Sarah shook her head slowly from side to side, and more tears fell. No job had ever excited her so much as singing in Matthew's saloon. It was like it was made for her, and her for it. That piano was hers—her fingers sailing over the keys making beautiful music, and her voice touching every person in the room. Well, every person except the drunks and the card players—most people, anyway.

A vibration in her pocket interrupted her thoughts. Oh! She had forgotten that her broken smartphone was in her pocket. It surprised her that it still worked after all that had happened. She fished it out of her pocket and looked at the screen. Someone had called, but she couldn't tell who. Hopefully, he or she had left a message on her home phone, as well. And now another chore— getting a new smartphone.

Sarah rode on until she came to the fence around Jenna's pasture. She opened the gate, walked through, and closed the gate. She exhaled slowly and frowned. Home sweet home, but it didn't feel like home anymore. The old Red Bluff felt more like home, but she couldn't return there. It's like they said, you can't go home again.

Sarah and Dancer walked across the pasture and through the open gate leading to the small corral outside the horses' stalls. Then she dismounted and walked Dancer into his stall. She unsaddled him, brushed him down by rote, and made sure there was hay in the automatic feeder before leaving the barn. Her heart wasn't in it. She just wanted to get on with her life—what was left of it, anyway. It felt like she had left her heart and soul behind in the old Red Bluff. No matter. She was here now, and she would deal with it whether she wanted to or not.

As she opened the door of her car, Madison came out of the house. "Hey, Sarah! I thought you were going to stay for two weeks."

"Hi, Madison. It didn't work out."

Madison could see that something was wrong. She put her hand on Sarah's arm. "Sarah, are you all right? Has something happened to Matthew?" Then her eyes got wide. "Jenna—has something happened to my Aunt Jenna or Granny?"

"No, Madison, everyone is fine. Nothing you have to worry about. I just went through a terrible ordeal that I can't talk about right now. But everyone in Red Bluff is good. I need to go home now, Madison. Good-bye."

Madison replied hesitantly, "You have marks on your face, Sarah. Is there anything I can do to help?"

"I'll be fine, thanks," said Sarah.

"Okay. Bye, Sarah."

As Sarah drove away, she could see Madison watching the car drive down the block. No matter. Madison was a good kid, but Sarah needed to get home. Home. Her condo wasn't home and would never feel like home again. But it was all she had right now.

She parked her car in the lot, walked to her condo, and unlocked the door. When she walked in, she realized that she had left her three bags in the old Red Bluff. Not that it mattered. She had plenty left for the Victorian Society. If she needed them, she could have Jenna bring them over next time she came this way. There were several gold coins among her belongings that would come in handy over here. Not that money meant anything to her at this point. Her life was a mess. A few gold coins wouldn't make it any better.

The phone rang, disturbing her thoughts. She thought about letting it ring through, then decided it was as good a time as any to come back to the real world.

"Hello," she said without enthusiasm.

"Hey, Sarah! Guess what! I've sold your condo! The guy came to see it Saturday and loved it so much that he made an offer immediately. Can you come over now to sign the papers?"

"Oh, hi, Gillian. Thank you, but I've changed my mind. I don't want to sell it right now."

"Ah, ah, Sarah," she said indignantly, "you can't get out of the contract. He's offering full price, you have to take it."

"No, I'm not going to."

"Sarah, are you all right? I know I don't know you very well, but you sound different."

"Yeah, I'm not all right. I just went through hell and back, and I'm not selling the condo. Okay?"

"Well, he did have one contingency. I'll tell him you refused it."

"Okay, bye." Sarah hung up without waiting for a reply. Then she walked into her bedroom, fell across the bed sideways, and cried herself to sleep.

CHAPTER THIRTY-THREE

SARAH AWOKE AT five in the morning, with her legs still hanging over the side of the bed, the taste of dirt in her mouth, and her heart heavy with regret. She had already decided what she was going to do. Although she had taken two weeks vacation, there was no way she was going to hang around thinking about everything she had lost. So, she'd go into work today, explain to Marcus that her plans had changed, and ask him if it was all right to return to work. She knew it would be all right with him. He may not be in love with her, but he did like her and respect her work. He would say it was fine.

Sarah showered and got ready for work, adding some makeup to hide the marks on her face. Except for her broken heart, it felt like any other day. But today, she wasn't going to allow herself to feel the dread that she had been feeling when getting ready for work the past few weeks. She couldn't afford to have those feelings now. Somehow she had to muster up the feelings of joy that her job used to bring her. Although much of that was just being around Marcus; and now without those feelings, there wasn't much joy to be had around there. But

126

she would try. She had to try.

After parking and locking her car, Sarah walked into the office. She greeted the receptionist, asked if Marcus was busy, walked down to his corner office, and knocked before entering.

"Sarah! I thought you were on vacation."

"Yes, Marcus, I was, but my plans have changed. Any chance I can come back to work now?"

"Sure, Sarah, arrange it with the woman who is taking your place. I think it's Amanda." With that, he looked down at his desk and continued his work.

Sarah breathed easier and walked down to her office to tell Amanda that she was to return to the secretarial pool. Amanda wouldn't mind—she was happy to do whatever anyone asked of her. Hmmm, thought Sarah. That's how I was when I first started.

After Amanda described to Sarah exactly what she had been working on, she walked out of the office and left Sarah alone with her work. Sarah felt grateful for the complex task that would keep her mind occupied for at least the rest of that day. She didn't want a minute of time to think about the loss of Matthew and her singing career.

The day raced by quickly. Before she knew it, it was already five o'clock. Sarah straightened everything up, powered down her computer, and left. She drove straight to the cell phone shop to get her phone replaced. Although she got there just before closing, they sold her the new unit and transferred all her information over. When she stepped back into the car, the new phone rang.

"Hello, Sarah," said Gillian, cautiously.

"Hello, Gillian. Did you take care of it for me?"

"I did, but the man really wants your condo. It's the

closet space—the extra closet space—he said it will be perfect for his wife. He offered the same price as before with no contingencies this time."

"I refuse the offer," said Sarah.

"I'm sorry, Sarah, you can't. You signed an exclusive right-to-sell agreement with us. This man is willing to pay the exact price you asked for with no contingencies. You can't say no."

"Crap," said Sarah. "There's nothing I can do?"

"No, Sarah, I'm sorry, nothing. He really wants it and he's willing to do whatever it takes to get it. You're kind of stuck," said Gillian. "You shouldn't have put it up for sale if you weren't ready," she added.

"I was ready!" shouted Sarah, then caught herself. "I'm sorry, Gillian, I've had a bad few days. I'm sorry that I yelled at you. I know it's not your fault. What do I have to do?"

"Come down to the office to sign the sales agreement. It will be a standard ninety-day escrow."

"I'll be down tomorrow. Bye."

Sarah clicked off the phone, pulled to the side of the road, and turned off her engine. Although she was less than five minutes from home, she had to stop. Sitting there and breathing deeply, she thought she could contain herself. But after a minute had passed, the tears flowed down her cheeks. She just sat there and let them flow.

Her real home in the old Red Bluff was out of her reach, and now where she lived in the new Red Bluff was about to be taken from her. It was more than she could handle. She wished she could talk to Jenna about this, but Jenna was in the old Red Bluff and unavailable to her. And there was no way she could go back there, even for just a short time. Anything could happen. And what had already happened was more than she could ever forget.

CHAPTER THIRTY-FOUR

MATTHEW FELT MISERABLE. He hadn't slept all night because he was going over all the events of the day before. He still blamed himself for what had happened to Sarah. Why couldn't he be more understanding? Then none of this would have happened. She'd be here beside him. She'd be safe.

Before walking downstairs, he stopped at Sarah's room. Opening the door, he stared into the room, taking in everything he had changed for her: the new curtains and bedspread, the clean rug, and the new toilet. Now that he knew she was from the future, he better understood the need for the toilet. Apparently, they didn't use outhouses in the future. He shook his head—thinking about outhouses at a time like this—just crazy. Then he noticed her three bags still sitting on the bed.

How would he get them back to her? She needed her clothes! What would she do without her clothes? He felt panicked. Walking into the room, he picked the bags up and put them down again. Then he picked them up again. And put them down.

"Matthew? What are you doing?" asked Zack.

Matthew looked up quickly. "Oh, I didn't hear you come in. I need to get these clothes to Sarah. How am I going to get them to her?" asked Matthew, still feeling anxious.

"Matthew, I don't think Sarah needs them. Haven't you noticed that she has never worn the same dress twice? I'm sure she has plenty of clothes. Besides, she'll be back! Don't worry, everything will work out, and Sarah will be back here before you know it!"

"I'm not as confident as you, Zack. I wish I were."

"It will work out, Matthew! It will! You have to trust that everything will work out. You have to!"

"All I know is that Sarah is not here. And there's no reason for me to believe that she will be here in the future." He hesitated after he realized what he said. "I mean—oh forget it."

Matthew walked past Zack, closed Sarah's door, and headed downstairs. He had gone into the kitchen to fix breakfast for the two of them, when he heard someone at the front door.

"I'll get it," said Zack.

As Matthew put more wood into the stove, he heard Josiah's voice. Then he heard Josiah and Zack walking toward the back.

"Matthew," said Josiah, "I need to talk to you about our plan."

Matthew stopped what he was doing to listen to Josiah. The plan to trap the other outlaws was his only hope of getting Sarah back.

"Yes, Josiah."

"I need you to go to my office tomorrow and ask about when the judge is coming to town. Act indignant. Mention that you want to see Sanford hang—you know, anything to spice it up."

"Is everything else in place?" asked Matthew.

"Yes, everything except—oh, can you do me a favor?" Josiah explained what he needed, and Matthew agreed to take care of it. Then Josiah said, "Listen, let's keep this plan to just the five of us, all right? Nick, you two, me, and Rawlins. The fewer people who know about this, the better. If word gets out, it could spoil all our plans." Matthew and Zack nodded, so Josiah continued. "There's one more item, Matthew. You need to get some bottles of whiskey ready for Rawlins."

"What?" asked Matthew. "I have plenty of whiskey, you know that."

"No, this is special whiskey. About this much whiskey," he held his thumb and forefinger an inch apart, "and the rest sarsaparilla. Give him the whole bottle, like you usually do, and he'll nurse it like he usually does. We have to still keep up appearances. Have some of those bottles ready, okay?"

"I can't believe Rawlins is willing to go along with this," said Matthew.

"He said he'd do it, and he's glad he can help. And I know what you're thinking—what if he messes up? It doesn't matter, the plan will still work. Don't worry, Matthew. But I think Rawlins can do this. So get the bottles ready, okay?"

"Yeah, sure," said Matthew. "I'll take care of it."

Josiah directed his next comment to Zack. "Zack, are you ready for this? A lot depends on you."

"I'm ready, Josiah. I'll do my best. I want to see Sarah again, and I feel like it depends on me whether she comes back or not."

"Not all of it, Zack, but yes, a lot does depend on you.

But we'll make this work. We have to," said Josiah. Then he turned and walked from the saloon.

The exchange with Josiah didn't make Matthew feel any better about his chances of getting Sarah back. If one part of the plan went wrong, then they would not only lose the rest of the gang, but they'd lose Sanford as well. If those outlaws were out loose, then it would be certain that Sarah would never return.

CHAPTER THIRTY-FIVE

SARAH STARTED HER car, drove home, and cried even more. She cried for so long and so hard that she didn't think that she would ever have any more tears left. But she wasn't just crying over the loss of the condo—everything that was important to her was being ripped from her. Admittedly, the condo wasn't that important to her. She had decided to sell it after all. Although that was when she thought she was moving to old Red Bluff. Now that she wasn't, it was a loss that she hadn't counted on.

The real issue, though, was Matthew. She had finally fallen for a good guy—a guy who respected her and treated her well. A guy who *loved* her—and a guy whom *she* loved. Sarah missed him so much, she couldn't stand it. And she missed singing, too. Sitting at that piano and singing, and having people clap and appreciate her and put tips in her glass—it was all so amazing—it was what she had always wanted. It was also something that had felt so far out of reach that she never even hoped for it. Then she had it—had it all—and now it was gone.

Sarah slept fitfully that night and awoke the next morning feeling tired and depressed. She lost her dream job, she lost her dream husband, and now she was losing her condo. At least she had three months to pack and get herself psyched up for leaving it. Now, what else could go wrong? She found out soon enough.

On her way to work, while stopped at a red light, her new smartphone rang. It was Gillian, the realtor.

"Hi, Sarah!"

"Hello, Gillian," said Sarah unenthusiastically.

"Have you accepted having your condo sold yet?"

"I've resigned myself to it, if that's what you mean. I'm not happy about it."

"Well, I have some news that might cheer you up!"

That perked Sarah up. "He's decided he doesn't want to buy my condo?"

"No, better than that! He wants to give you twenty thousand more dollars for it!"

"Give me twenty thousand more, huh? What's the catch?" The last thing on Sarah's mind right now was money.

"A thirty-day escrow. But wait! Before you say it's too soon, it's not! I have some neighbors who would love to help you pack and move. This is a no-brainer, Sarah, you have to do it."

Sarah sighed. For Gillian, it was all about the money. For Sarah, she just wanted the nightmare to be over. And selling her condo when she didn't want to sell it, was the latest installment of her current nightmare. If she wanted it to be over, then thirty days would work. Why not? She also didn't have the strength to argue with Gillian. Obviously that was what *she* wanted.

"Yes, Gillian, fine. Whatever you say."

"Okay! All right! Good decision, Sarah! This will be great. So, you'll stop by my office on your way home tonight? I'll have the new contract all ready for you!"

"Yeah, fine, bye." Sarah hung up the smartphone, pulled into the lot, and parked her car.

Back at her desk again, Sarah finished the complex work and was left with some mundane tasks that didn't hold her interest—or her thoughts. All she could think about was Matthew and Red Bluff. Even her singing took second place to wanting to be with Matthew. She needed a break, so she put down her pencil and walked to the break room.

Chad was in there getting some coffee. Stepping to the side, she patiently waited until he finished pouring his. Then he saw her.

"Sarah! Great to see you! I thought you were on vacation this week or something."

"Something came up. I canceled it."

"Oh, well, glad you're back. You want to go to dinner tonight? I have an opening."

Oh, no, thought Sarah. Did he actually say he had an opening? "No, sorry, Chad, I'm busy."

"How about tomorrow night or Friday?"

Sarah tried not to laugh—thinking that it sounded like he had lots of openings. How would she get out of this now? Ah, the truth. "I'm sorry, Chad, I'm in love with someone." The words surprised even Sarah, but they just flowed out of her mouth.

Chad didn't know what to say. For once. "In love? Wow, we just went out a couple of weeks ago. It must have been sudden."

"Long story," said Sarah.

"Oh," said Chad, "somebody from the past, huh?"

Sarah smiled a vacant smile and slapped her hand on the counter. "Yes, Chad! That's exactly right! Somebody from the past!" And then she started laughing uproariously and couldn't stop.

Her behavior made Chad uncomfortable, so he didn't say anything more and walked out of the room. That made Sarah laugh even harder. She laughed so hard, that she slid down onto the floor, still laughing uncontrollably. There she sat, on the dirty floor, with her fancy dress and shoes to match, laughing so hard that tears began flowing down her cheeks.

She didn't know how long she sat there like that, or how many people peeked in the doorway to see what was up, but finally, Cynthia, the office manager, came in. Cynthia knelt down by Sarah and looked at her.

"Sarah? Are you okay?"

"No," said Sarah.

"Sarah, I think you should go home now. Can you drive yourself, or do you need someone to drive you?"

"I can drive."

"Can I help you get up?" asked Cynthia.

Sarah nodded her head and gave her hand to Cynthia, who helped pull her up. Then she hugged Cynthia and said, "Thank you." Cynthia walked her to the exit and watched as Sarah walked to her car and drove away.

CHAPTER THIRTY-SIX

As MATTHEW WALKED toward the sheriff's office, he allowed himself to get all worked up. He didn't have to pretend to be indignant, because he did want to see Sanford hanged. After what he did to Sarah—and after what he almost did—he deserved to hang. Matthew grabbed the handle on the door and charged in.

"Where's Josiah?" asked Matthew in an elevated voice to make sure Sanford could hear it.

"Hi, Matthew. Josiah isn't here right now."

"I want to know when that no-account animal will be hanged!" Matthew stepped back, walked to the door to the cells, and peered in. "Oh, you've moved him."

"Josiah didn't want him near Rawlins."

"That makes sense. So when will he be hanged?" Matthew demanded.

"You need to be patient, Matthew. Josiah has already arranged everything, and he said he expects the judge to be here Saturday morning."

"Great! The sooner the better!" said Matthew.

"Hey, you! Your woman had really sweet lips, you know that?" asked Sanford.

Matthew fumed, but didn't say a word. He knew the man was piling on the agony just to get to him. It was all he could do to stand still and ignore the comment. Then he heard Nick's chair move.

"You know what she said to me? She told me that she liked kissing me better 'n kissing you!" said Sanford.

Matthew rushed into the cell room toward Sanford, but Nick caught him from behind holding him back. Matthew struggled to get out of his grasp, but Nick held tight.

"Matthew, he's saying that to provoke you. You know that. Come on, let it go. The judge will be here soon, and it will be over." Nick led him toward the door. "Go now, it will be over soon."

Still fuming, Matthew turned and walked out the door, slamming it behind him. Although Matthew knew Sanford's words were not true—Matthew had never even kissed Sarah—the words bothered him because it made the whole nightmare real again. He stood there in front of the door for a few minutes trying to settle himself.

Everything depended on this wild plan. Matthew felt like his whole life depended on the plan. Sarah was his life now, and if she couldn't return, he had no idea how he would live without her.

Matthew walked next door to the general store. When he entered, he saw that no one else was in there. He called out, "Ryan? You here?"

"Be right out, Matthew. Gimme a minute, here."

When Ryan walked out from the back a few minutes later, Matthew noticed that he had some paint on his hands and a dab of it on his chin.

"You've got paint on your chin, Ryan."

"Ah, part of the hazards of being a painter! What can

I do for you, Matthew?"

"Is anyone else in the back? Or are we alone here?"

Ryan looked concerned. "We're alone, Matthew, what's up?"

Matthew explained to him exactly what he needed and why. Then he told Ryan to keep it a secret—because Sarah's life depended on it. "Can you get that for me, then?" asked Matthew.

"I don't have anything here like that," said Ryan. "But I know where I can get it," and he winked at Matthew. When Matthew didn't respond, Ryan said, "You know, don't you? I mean—"

Matthew nodded his head. "Yes, Ryan, I know about the future."

"All right, good. I thought you did. I'll take care of this tomorrow. I need to arrange with Jenna to watch the store for me, but it shouldn't be a problem. And then I'll go back, take care of that, and I'll talk to Sarah, too. Tell her what's going on here and that she should be able to come back soon."

"Thanks, Ryan, I appreciate that," said Matthew. He turned to go, then turned back. "Can you give her a message for me, please? Will you tell her that I love her more than I can say?"

Ryan smiled and nodded his head. "I'll tell 'er for ya, Matthew."

Matthew plodded back to the saloon not any happier than when he left. Zack had restocked the bar and had gotten everything ready for the day, which Matthew was grateful for.

"Thanks, Zack. I'm going upstairs. Can you handle it in here?"

"Matthew, I can handle it, but I don't think it's good

for you to mope around. You'd be better off staying busy," said Zack.

Matthew put his hand on Zack's shoulder. "You've become a good man and a good friend, Zack. I thank you for that. But I don't feel like standing at this bar today."

"What are you going to do upstairs?"

"Go into Sarah's room and see if there's anything else that I can fix up for her in there."

Now it was Zack's turn to reach up and put his hand on Matthew's shoulder. With a concerned look on his face, he said, "Matthew, I'm worried about you."

"I'll be okay, Zack." Matthew paused. "When Sarah comes back." He looked around the saloon at the handful of men. "And she'll be back after that man gets hanged. Thanks again, Zack. I'll be upstairs." Then he turned and walked slowly up the stairs.

CHAPTER THIRTY-SEVEN

SARAH WAS NOT embarrassed at what had happened the day before. It was more like she was horrified. And it wasn't that it had happened at work that bothered her. It was that her life had come to that. She could admit it now—her life was out of control. As much as she hated it, she had to admit it. Now, what was she going to do about it? That was the real question.

Chad avoided her when he saw her in the break room. Cynthia asked how she felt and then dropped it, for which Sarah was very grateful. Let them think it was PMS or something. She didn't care what they thought. She only cared about what she was going to do to fix it.

That day, another complex assignment kept her busy all day. Before leaving, though, she went to the copy room and picked up as many empty boxes as she could manage to get out the door. Moving had become a priority—granted, it was an unwanted one—but a priority, nonetheless.

She drove home and was unloading the last of the boxes, when her smartphone rang. Since she didn't recognize the number, she let the call go to voicemail and brought the boxes inside the house. Then she listened to the voicemail.

"Hey, Sarah! It's Ryan. I need to talk to you. I'm not going to be here much longer. Please call me back as soon as you can."

As the phone on the other end rang, Sarah wondered why Ryan would be calling her—why had he even returned to her Red Bluff? Was Jenna okay? Granny? Matthew? Her thoughts were interrupted when he answered his phone.

"Hello!"

"Hi, Ryan. What's up? Is everything all right?"

"More or less. Matthew feels devastated that you're gone and devastated about what happened to you. He told me to tell you that he loves you."

Sarah blinked her eyes trying to keep from crying. "Tell him that I love him, too."

"I will, Sarah, I will. What I'm calling about is because they have a plan to catch the rest of the gang. I don't know all the details, they're keeping hush-hush about it, but Matthew asked me to get them something that could be dropped on the trail and followed, but not obvious if you weren't looking for it. They were thinking of some large beads, but I bought some white garden gravel instead. It should be perfect for what they're looking for."

"Something dropped on the trail—sounds like Hansel and Gretel! But I don't know how that's going to help them find Lucius and the others."

"I don't know, either. I'll just give it to them and see how it goes. Matthew said it would only be two more days before the plan begins. I thought you'd want to know—you know, in case you were ready to come back to the old Red Bluff."

143

"I'd love to come back, Ryan, but even with all the gang caught, how could I ever feel safe there again?"

"Sarah, have you ever been car-jacked?"

"No."

"What do you think would happen if someone from the past came here and happened to get car-jacked? They'd never want to return, right? And what are the real chances that it would ever happen again? Yes, there are dangers in the old Red Bluff that aren't here. I'll give you that. But right now you're trading your love in for fear. You're letting fear control you. You're letting fear win."

Sarah was silent for a minute while she took all his words in. "You're right, Ryan. I knew my life was out of control, but I couldn't explain why. It's the fear. I have been letting it control me and stop me from living my best life. You're absolutely right."

"Sarah, I will—or someone will—let you know if the plan is successful."

Sarah allowed herself to hope for the first time since her return. "I have a feeling that it will be, Ryan. I really do. Thank you for telling me all this."

"No problem, Sarah, no problem. How is everything else going?"

"Everything in the new Red Bluff sucks! I still can't stand my job, and now I have to move out of my condo in a month. I have no idea where I can live."

"Well, Sarah, I'm considering that wherever you live, it's going to be temporary, anyway. So, why don't I ask Madison if you can move in with her for a while? How about that?"

"That'd be awesome, Ryan! Do you really think she'll say yes?"

144

"I'm almost sure of it, Sarah. I think she's a little lonely in this big house all by herself."

"Thanks, Ryan. Thanks for everything."

"Sarah, good-bye, and I'll see you soon!"

"I hope so, Ryan. Thanks, and bye."

CHAPTER THIRTY-EIGHT

SARAH SMILED WHEN she got off the phone with Ryan. The smile felt funny on her face—as if she hadn't smiled in a while. And indeed, she had not. And she found that it felt good. She liked to smile, and it was good to feel happy again—or at least to have some hope.

After eating a quick dinner, she began organizing some of her belongings. She separated everything that she might need anytime soon. Need? Need where? At Madison's or the old Red Bluff? And would Madison even agree to let her stay there? As if in answer to that, her phone rang.

"Hello?"

"Hey, Sarah! It's Madison. Listen, Ryan just left and told me that you might need a temporary place to stay. You're welcome to stay here. This house is so big that I've been bouncing off the walls alone here. There's plenty of room. Stay as long as you want!"

"Madison, that's awesome." Tears came into Sarah's eyes at Madison's warm invitation, and she fought to keep them out of her voice. "I can't tell you how much I appreciate it."

"Sarah, Ryan told me what happened to you. Wow, it sounds awful. I'm so sorry."

"It's okay. I'm recovering quickly."

"And I understand why you don't want to go back right now, but it sounds like they're going to catch the guys who did it. Then you can go back, right?"

"I hope it happens, and I hope I can go back, Madison. I just hope I can."

"Okay, well you're welcome to move in anytime. I'm in the back bedroom, so don't take that one, and Jenna and Josiah still stay occasionally, so don't take her room, but you can choose either of the other two."

"Wait. Jenna *and* Josiah stay there occasionally? Is that what you said?"

"Well, yeah. They've come a few times is all. But Jenna said they'd be back. Listen, Sarah, I have to get back to my homework now. So, come over and move in whenever you want. See ya! Bye!"

"Bye," said Sarah absentmindedly. Jenna and Josiah? Why would they come back to the new Red Bluff? That didn't make much sense to her. She'd have to ask Jenna about it the next time she saw her. Whenever that was.

Immediately, she began feverishly packing boxes. It needed to be taken care of, and the sooner her condo was all packed up, the sooner this part of the nightmare would be over. And now that she definitely had a place to stay, she could proceed without having to worry about that part of it, anyway.

Sarah worked far into the night, fell asleep exhausted, and awoke the next morning filled with hope. She felt better than she had since she returned to her own time. Finally, she could consider returning to sing at the saloon, living in the old Red Bluff, and most of all, returning to her love, Matthew. The plan to catch the rest of the gang—especially Lucius—had to work. It just had to.

At work, after she finished the project that she was working on, she walked into the break room to refill her coffee. As she came out with her coffee cup full, she ran into Marcus, who had been looking for her.

"Ah, Sarah, there you are." He held out a stub to her. "Can you pick up my cleaning for me sometime today? I need it for tomorrow."

Sarah didn't reach out her hand, but instead looked into his eyes and tilted her head. Impatient, Marcus shook the stub at her. She put her coffee cup down on the desk she was walking by, looked at the stub without touching it, and shook her head.

"No, Marcus, I won't pick up your dry cleaning."

Marcus, taken aback, said, "What? What do you mean you won't?"

"I mean, I'm finished. I quit. You can pick up your cleaning by yourself! Good-bye!"

Then she walked past him, picked up her things from her office, and quickly strutted out the front door of the office with her head held high. Walking to her car, she looked back at the building she had just come out of. The years I worked there have mostly been good, thought Sarah. And now I'm done, forevermore.

CHAPTER THIRTY-NINE

MATTHEW HANDED RAWLINS another bottle of the watered-down whiskey and grumbled. He grumbled because he always grumbled when he gave Rawlins whiskey. But this time, it was a fake grumble. As far as he knew, Rawlins had been nearly sober for three days running now, but still acted drunk. Matthew had to give him credit for that. For one thing, he played the part beautifully, and even fell asleep at the table a time or two. For the second thing, he had actually stayed sober.

As he grumbled, Matthew's heart leaped with joy. From the beginning, he had felt the part of the plan that was the weakest was the part that involved Rawlins. Now, he felt sure the plan would succeed and Sarah would return to him. Still, a lot had to go right for the plan to succeed, but he felt this was a good omen.

Matthew couldn't believe the time for the plan was almost there. A few more hours and they would begin. Knowing they would be up most of the night, Matthew and Zack had taken turns upstairs, so they could try to get a little sleep. He wasn't sure about Zack, but it didn't work well for Matthew. All the possibilities kept rolling around in his head as he tried to sleep. He imagined that Zack had even more possibilities rolling around in *his* head.

The hours passed quickly. Matthew knew what was happening at the sheriff's office. Josiah was over there telling of past successes to Nick to keep Sanford from trying something too early. Josiah would leave shortly. And then when the saloon closed, Rawlins would stumble back to the jail where Nick would pretend to be sleeping. Then Rawlins would grab the keys hoping Sanford would notice and entice him into the cell next to his. That was also a critical part to the plan.

Since there were often horses in front of the saloon, they would leave Dolly there. That was Jenna's idea. Dolly was a great horse, but she was slow. It could only work in their favor for Sanford to have a slow horse. Jenna said that if she didn't get Dolly back, she'd never forgive them.

After everyone left the saloon at the regular closing time, Matthew looked out through the swinging doors and saw Dolly tied to the hitching rail. Satisfied, Matthew stepped back and closed the door. Zack had left a half hour earlier to be ready for his part. Now Matthew buckled his gun belt and headed out the back door where his horse was waiting for him. He slipped the rifle into the scabbard and took off.

Matthew's post was closest to town. It was his job to report if nothing happened, or if Sanford never passed him on his way out of town. But how long was he supposed to wait? They had never discussed that. So Matthew sat with his back against one tree and remained hidden by another tree and several bushes. But he had maneuvered himself into a position where he could see the road perfectly. See but not be seen. Perfect.

More than an hour had passed, but Matthew wasn't sleepy at all. If anything, he was increasingly vigilant. If Sarah was ever to return to Red Bluff—his Red Bluff—this plan had to work. It had to. He hoped that Zack was also wide awake, but he felt confident that he was. Zack had been looking forward to this. He felt nervous that so much depended on him, but also felt good that Josiah had so much confidence in him. Zack wouldn't let him down.

Matthew heard a noise coming down the road, and he straightened to see it better. A deer. A big, fat buck walked down the middle of the road, pretty as you please. He would have laughed if he didn't need to be silent. As Matthew relaxed back against the tree, he heard another sound. Clip-clop, clip-clop. A trotting horse.

When the horse came into view, he could see that it was Dolly with Sanford riding. Matthew closed his eyes and sighed deeply. It was working. It was working. He couldn't believe it.

The plan was, if Dolly passed by at a run, then Matthew would follow in ten minutes. If Dolly passed by at a trot, Matthew would wait fifteen minutes before following. And hopefully, by that time, Nick would arrive from the jail. Josiah would be farther down the road, following the same general plan.

Zack, even farther down the line, had the most important job. He would follow the same plan, although by then, everyone expected Dolly would be going as quick as greased lightning. Zack would follow—not close enough for Sanford to see him or hear him—but he would be responsible for staying on Sanford's trail. The

151

plan wouldn't have worked at all, except they were blessed with a full moon.

And Zack had one more responsibility. His saddlebags were filled with the white gravel that Ryan had brought back from the future. He was to drop one or two pieces of gravel every so often, so the rest of the posse would know they were on the right trail. And if there was a turn off, he would drop several pieces so the markers wouldn't be missed. Josiah said he had come up with the idea because of a fairy tale that he had read when he was a child.

The minutes ticked by. Another horse approached from down the road. Matthew walked back to retrieve his horse and waited in the bushes until he was sure it was Nick. When he saw that it was, Matthew walked out to the road and climbed into the saddle.

"So he was trotting, then?" whispered Nick.

"Yes."

"He won't be for long. Let's get going." Nick urged his horse forward, and they were off.

Matthew wasn't sure he was horseman enough to control his horse and keep him at a reasonable distance, but luckily, his horse followed Nick's lead. Now the adventure had really begun.

CHAPTER FORTY

SARAH SANG ALL the way home. She couldn't stop singing. She sang "She Loves You," "Achy Breaky Heart," and "Moon River." When she pulled into her parking place at her condo, she turned off the engine and finished singing the chorus to "Take This Job and Shove It." Then she walked to her door with a smile spread across her face.

Walking inside, she kicked off her shoes and lay down on her couch, still dressed. She yelled into the room, "I'm free! I'm free! I'm free!" And started singing all her favorite songs, and then all the songs from the past that she sang in the old Red Bluff.

She kept singing loud and strong until the door bell interrupted her. Sarah didn't know who it was and didn't care. She wanted to spend the evening by herself, celebrating in her own way. Celebrate quitting her job, selling her condo, and moving back to the old Red Bluff to be with Matthew. Wait! What day is it? When was the plan supposed to happen? What if Ryan was at the door to tell her the plan had failed? She jumped up and ran to the door, as the bell rang again.

Throwing open the door, she felt relieved to see that it was Gillian, holding a bunch of boxes, with more boxes scattered around her. Sarah smiled at her and motioned her inside.

"I come bearing gifts," said Gillian. She walked in with the boxes she was carrying, while Sarah stepped out the door and brought the rest inside.

"Thank you, Gillian! I appreciate that!"

"You look absolutely radiant, Sarah! You're not mad at me anymore for selling your condo?"

"Mad? I couldn't be happier!" Sarah said and gave Gillian a big hug.

"Oh, that's good. I didn't want you to be angry with me. This really was a great opportunity with the market as it is. It's recovering, you know, but still slow."

"Whatever, Gillian, I'm just glad I don't have to worry about renting it or something after I move."

"Oh! Where are you moving to?"

Oops, thought Sarah, shouldn't have revealed so much. "Well, for now, out to the edge of town, where my horse is. After that, not sure." It was true. She wasn't positive about going back to Red Bluff. Although she hoped to, until they caught the outlaws, she couldn't.

"I didn't know you had a horse. Well, anyway, here are the boxes. I thought you could use them. Would you like me to help you pack? I'd be happy to."

"No thanks, Gillian. I appreciate you bringing the boxes. Most of it is organized, but I had used all my boxes last night and forgot to get more today."

"Do you think you could use more?" asked Gillian.

"You've seen my 'closet room.' I still have all my clothes to pack."

"Oh, Sarah, you should get some wardrobe boxes

from a mover. Then you can hang all your clothes up, and they won't wrinkle."

"That's a great idea, Gillian! I had never thought about that. I haven't moved in so long. I'll do that tomorrow! Thanks! And thanks for stopping by!"

"No problem, Sarah. Good luck on your packing."

"Bye now."

Sarah looked around at all the empty boxes on the floor and beamed. It was true. It was all happening. She had left her job, which she hadn't been able to stand for months—since falling out of love with Marcus—and now she was free to do what she wanted to do. And what she wanted to do was move to the old Red Bluff and be with Matthew. Although that depended on if the plan to catch the outlaws worked.

CHAPTER FORTY-ONE

MATTHEW AND NICK continued riding down the road. When they passed where Josiah had been hiding, Nick nodded his head at Matthew.

"Josiah's gone, let's kick it up a notch." Nick urged his horse again, and the horse bounded ahead, with Matthew following.

As they passed where Zack was to hide out, Nick said, "Let's start looking for the gravel now. Oh, right there, see it?"

"Yeah, see it," said Matthew.

Time and miles wore on. Nick pulled up his horse to a walk. "They've been running too long. They need a rest."

"We won't lose Sanford, will we? I don't want to leave Zack and Josiah without help."

"I'm sure Zack and Josiah will be resting their horses, too. We've been at this for a while."

Matthew, thinking of Jenna's horse, Dolly, hoped that Sanford wouldn't hurt her. Dolly was a good horse, and Matthew didn't want anything to happen to her. He may not be a real horseman, but he was fond of horses.

After some time, Nick urged his horse to trot. Matthew didn't like the trot much—he wasn't a good enough rider to know how to handle it—but he was glad they were speeding up. He didn't want to get left behind.

Whenever Nick saw a piece of white gravel, he silently pointed it out to Matthew, and Matthew did the same. Soon, Nick pressed his horse into a canter, and Matthew's horse followed. Earlier, they had passed the trail to the cabin where they had rescued Sarah. Matthew knew the other gang members wouldn't go back there, but he hoped the new hiding place would be close. He wanted this over as soon as possible, so he could get word to Sarah that it was safe for her to return.

The road forked up ahead. A steady stream of gravel led to the right. After they were on the new trail for a few minutes, Nick spoke.

"I think Zack has slowed down."

"What makes you think so?" asked Matthew.

"Just a feeling. But I've learned to trust my feelings." He shifted his weight, and with a slight movement of his hands, the horse slowed. Matthew's horse, grateful for the rest, slowed too much, and Matthew had to nudge him to catch up with Nick.

They hadn't been on the new trail long when Matthew spotted several pieces of white gravel leading to a deer trail. He pointed at it, and Nick nodded his head.

"Good catch, Matthew. I would've missed that one."

Turning onto the new trail, Nick slowed his horse into a trot. They rode single file on the narrow path. Matthew thought they must be getting close. He wondered where Josiah and Zack were. He hoped they were both safe.

Suddenly, a man stepped out from the cover of trees onto the trail in front of Nick. It was Josiah, and he

157

motioned them to stop.

"I caught a glimpse of Zack just up ahead. He's walking his horse. He's either lost the trail, or else we're close. I think Sanford is around here, I can smell him.

"I don't think we should leave the horses here, in case this is just a rest or something," continued Josiah. "Let's walk 'em slowly and see what we find." Josiah slipped back into the heavy growth and led his horse out onto the trail.

When Matthew and Nick saw that Josiah meant lead the horses, they dismounted. Matthew grabbed his rifle from the scabbard, because he wanted to be ready if anything happened. If something *was* going to happen, he felt that it would be soon.

Josiah walked in front with his gun drawn. Nick followed with his gun drawn. And Matthew came up behind them, with his rifle ready. As they came around a corner, Josiah stopped unexpectedly.

"Back, back," whispered Josiah.

Men and horses backed up, and Josiah motioned for them to leave their horses there in the woods. After securing them to some trees, Josiah led the way to the right of the path. Through the trees, with branches brushing against his face and clothes, Matthew followed Nick and Josiah.

A few minutes later, Josiah knelt down and motioned that they should, too. As he knelt, Matthew could see in front of him directly through the underbrush. There was a cabin, with five horses tied out in front. One of them was Dolly.

Matthew felt conflicting emotions of relief and terror. This was only the beginning. What happened from this point on would determine Matthew's fate—with Sarah or without her. He swallowed hard and made sure his rifle was loaded and ready. But wait. Where was Zack?

CHAPTER FORTY-TWO

TWO HOURS, FIVE boxes, and much organization later, Sarah sat on the couch amazed at her progress. Since she already had three full bags of old-time clothes waiting for her at the saloon, she didn't need many more. Just another bag or two would do. And since Matthew planned on doing all the cooking, she didn't need to bring any cooking utensils like when Jenna moved her stuff into her ranch there. Ah, Sarah thought, how wonderful to have a man who cooks! She sighed. But he wasn't her man, yet. Not until she moved back there. And she hoped that would happen soon.

Sarah drank the last of the hot chocolate and brought the cup into the kitchen to rinse it. A decadent pleasure. That's how she looked at hot chocolate. But she deserved it, so she enjoyed every drop. As she rinsed the glass, her doorbell rang. Glancing at the clock, she thought it was late for anyone to stop by unannounced. Probably someone selling something, thought Sarah.

She would've ignored it, but the bell rang again. Leaning into the door, she looked out the peephole. She gasped and backed up quickly. Then she unlocked the door and opened it.

"Marcus!" she exclaimed.

"Hello, Sarah. May I come in." It wasn't a question and he pushed his way past her. The undeniable smell of alcohol followed him.

"Um, Marcus, you've been drinking." Sarah closed the door behind him.

"A little." He turned toward her and put his hands on her shoulders. "Sarah. You need to come back. I miss you. I need you."

"Marcus," she said, as she tried unsuccessfully to back out of his grasp, "I haven't even been gone one full day."

"Yes, I know, but this time you're not coming back." He dropped his hands to his sides and looked down. "When you were on vacation, I knew you would be back."

Sarah stayed silent. She didn't know what to say to him. She also didn't know if she wanted to ask him to sit down. His presence there made her uncomfortable.

"Sarah," Marcus continued, "if it's the cleaning, I'll get someone else to do it. Honest. I didn't think you minded it. For a long time I thought you *liked* it."

"For a long time, I did like it."

"I'm sorry that I didn't notice when you stopped liking it. Had I known that, I would have arranged something else. Asked another girl. I'm sorry. Please come back, Sarah. Please."

"Marcus, I didn't leave because of the cleaning. That was just one *more* reason to leave. I don't like the job anymore. I haven't liked it since I—well, I just don't like it anymore." She wasn't about to tell him that she used to be in love with him.

"I care about you, Sarah."

"What?" asked Sarah, confused.

Marcus reached for her, and Sarah took a step backward. "I care about you, Sarah. You're important to me." He stepped toward her.

Sarah held out her arms defensively. "Marcus, I don't know where you're going with this, but you've been drinking. Don't forget that you're happily married."

"Was," said Marcus.

"What do you mean, 'was'?"

"I mean she left me a few months ago."

"I'm sorry to hear that, Marcus."

"Are you, Sarah?" He quickly took a step forward and grabbed Sarah's hands before she could resist. "I always thought you were attracted to me."

She tried pulling her hands away, but he held on tight. "I may have been, but not anymore." As soon as she said it, she knew it had been a mistake to admit that.

"Oh, Sarah," he dropped her hands and in one fluid movement stepped closer and wrapped his arms around her. Before she could even resist, he had planted his lips on hers.

She forcefully pushed him away and slapped him. "No! Once I was attracted to you, but *no more*! I'm in love with someone else! Leave me alone. Get out of my apartment! Now!" She walked toward the door and opened it.

"Can't we talk about this, Sarah? If I hadn't already been married, you would have been the one. I swear it. I always thought you were beautiful. I want you."

"Marcus, get out of my apartment. There's nothing to talk about. And I'm not coming back." When Marcus still lingered, she added, "*Get—out—now!*"

Marcus walked out of the apartment, immediately turned around, and was about to speak when Sarah closed the door in his face. After locking the door, she leaned against it, exhaled, and said, "Whew!"

CHAPTER FORTY-THREE

JOSIAH LOOKED AROUND and said, "Where's Zack? Do either of you see Zack?"

Matthew said, "I was wondering the same thing."

"I don't see him," said Nick.

The three men watched the cabin. There was movement inside, but no movement outside.

"What's the plan, Josiah?" asked Nick.

"I'm concerned that we haven't seen Zack," said Josiah. "But I guess we can't wait. Maybe he's around back. You two stay here, and I'll go around to the left." Josiah, leaning over and close to the ground, walked back far enough the way they had come so he could cross the trail without being seen.

Matthew and Nick continued watching the cabin in silence. Someone stood at the window looking out. No other movement, not even Josiah, could be seen.

"Oh, wait, look at that," said Nick. He chuckled.

Matthew looked around and didn't see anything at first. Then he noticed that Dolly was untying the rope that kept her restrained. Working at it, working at it, working at it—Dolly finally had herself free. Now she had turned to the right and was heading in that direction. And she was heading straight for Zack, who was quietly calling her.

"Ah-oh," said Nick.

Matthew noticed the door of the cabin had opened and someone had come out.

"Get your rifle ready," said Nick. "When he sees Zack —"

Before Matthew could even lift his rifle, the man had seen Zack. He was the man in the saloon that Sarah had poured whiskey on! Matthew set his jaw, but before he could aim his gun, Nick had reached behind and pulled a gun from under his shirt. Matthew had never seen anything like it.

Zack was oblivious to the man about to pull a gun on him. He had his gun drawn, but it was pointed to the ground as he used his left hand to entice Dolly toward him.

Matthew knew he couldn't get his rifle up and aimed in time to save Zack. Next thing he knew, a terrible blast sounded, along with another shot, and the outlaw lay on the ground.

Matthew thought that Josiah had shot him at the same time Nick shot him. But when he looked at Zack, the poor kid was lying on the ground grasping his arm. Matthew started to stand up to go get him, when Nick pulled him back down.

"No, wait." Nick made a low whistling sound that attracted Zack's attention. Zack scrambled on the ground to get his gun and put it back into his holster. Then he waited for Dolly to meander over to him, and he pulled her into the overgrowth behind him. A few minutes later, Zack was with them.

165

The sound behind them made all three men turn. Josiah had returned.

"Zack, you okay?" he asked.

"He got me in my right arm. Now I can't shoot," said Zack.

"Let me look," said Nick. "It's bleeding badly. We need to stop the bleeding." He reached down, pulled his pants leg up, and uncurled a piece of fabric from his ankle. "Here, let me put this on. It should help slow down the blood."

"What is that?" asked Matthew, who had never seen fabric like that before.

"It's called an ace bandage. My ankle's been sore—that's why it's on there, but it will work well as a bandage without cutting off the circulation."

"Okay," said Josiah. "Zack is okay. They know we are here. First thing we need to do is get their horses out of there. We don't want a repeat of what happened last time."

"I'll go," said Zack.

"You're hurt!" said Matthew.

"I can't shoot a gun, but I can untie horses," said Zack. "I'm the obvious one to go. All of you need to shoot."

"He's right," said Josiah. "Okay, Zack. Be careful. Go back this way," he pointed behind him, "far enough so you can cross the trail without being seen. It's not far. Untie the horses, one at a time, starting with the one closest to the edge. If you need to, draw your gun with your left hand. *They* don't know you can't shoot left-handed. We'll cover you."

Zack slinked off behind them. Matthew watched until Zack was out of sight. Besides seeing shadows in the

166

window, there was no other movement anywhere around. A couple of minutes later, he could see Zack untie the first horse and then the second. He had trouble undoing the knot on the third horse, but finally managed.

All three men had their guns pointed toward the cabin. As Zack started to untie the fourth horse, the cabin door opened. All three men fired toward the door, and the man fell before he ever stepped out. Someone broke open the window and began firing at them. They returned fire and heard a scream.

Zack had dropped to the ground and was leaning against the cabin wall, while the frightened horse pulled back and paced from side to side at the end of the rope that held him. When there was a break in the gunfire, Zack crawled back over to the last horse trying to untie the rope. The other horses had moved off a few paces and grazed at some grass by the edge of the cabin.

The door of the cabin opened suddenly. While Nick and Josiah shot over his head—expecting someone to walk out—a man crawled quickly out, grabbed Zack from behind, and put a gun to his head. Then he stood up and laughed.

It was Sanford. "I've got your boy! And I will kill him unless you do exactly as I say. You will let me get on this horse and ride away." He kept talking, but Matthew couldn't focus on his words. As much as he wanted Sarah to be with him, he did not want it at the expense of Zack's life. Josiah's voice interrupted his thoughts.

"Matthew, can you shoot him from here without hitting Zack?" Josiah whispered.

The rifle was shaking so much that Matthew couldn't even answer. Nick, unseen behind the trees, and with his strange gun held straight out in front of him, said, "I've got it," and fired his gun.

Another terrible blast, and when Matthew looked again, both Sanford and Zack were on the ground. Matthew cried out, but before he could even stand, he saw that Zack was struggling to get up one-handed. Pinned beneath Sanford, Zack had to push him off. He stood up and raised his good arm in triumph.

"Get back!" said Josiah. "There might still be someone alive in the cabin."

Matthew counted. Five men altogether. The man who went after Dolly, and Sanford, both as cold as a wagon tire. The man who had come out the door first, probably dead. That left two more possibly alive.

"Nick, you want to come with me?" asked Josiah.

"You bet," said Nick.

"Matthew, you stay here and cover us."

Matthew, his gun still shaking but not as much, mumbled yes and put his finger on the trigger. Josiah and Nick, each moving off in opposite directions, came at the cabin from different sides. Zack had moved away from the front of the cabin to get out of the way. Matthew took a deep breath and held the gun steady as he saw Josiah and Nick, crouched down, approach the front of the cabin.

Nick arrived at the door first and pushed it open, still standing outside. Josiah came from the other side, and they walked into the cabin back to back, each with his gun drawn.

"All clear!" yelled Josiah.

Zack went back to untying the final horse at the hitching rail, and Matthew stood up and walked toward the cabin. When he went in, he didn't like what he saw.

Three men. One with a bullet through the middle of his chest, dead. Two others, badly hurt. One looked like he could die any second. The other struggled for breath with another chest wound.

For Matthew, it was over. He stepped back outside, walked to the edge of the cabin, leaned against the corner, and broke down in tears. Zack would be all right. Josiah and Nick were fine. The outlaws were either dead or about to be dead. It was safe. Sarah could come home now. Home to him.

CHAPTER FORTY-FOUR

SARAH AWOKE, STRETCHED, and smiled at the freedom of her new existence. Her condo sold, no job that she couldn't stand going to—oh. That reminded her of Marcus's visit the night before. How ironic that he should declare his love to her now. She had been in love with him for years, and he had showed no interest in her. Now, after she had let go of the fantasy and coincidentally Marcus's wife had left him, he comes on to her. What an interesting twist, she thought.

Her mind wandered into a fantasy of what it might be like being married to Marcus. Living in a big, beautiful house, a housekeeper to cook and clean for her, plenty of expensive clothes to wear, and going to exclusive parties that others could only dream about. Then reality struck —living with a man whose job was more important to him than she was.

And Matthew, she smiled at the thought of him. Humble, sweet, kind Matthew. He would cook for her, and instead of it being a job, he would cook for her with love in his heart.

Now that she had the choice of a rich, comfortable

existence with Marcus, could she give that up for a simple life with Matthew? The doorbell rang. Thinking it was Gillian with more boxes for her, she lingered in bed a minute longer to consider. Oh, yes, the simple life with Matthew is what she would choose. That may not have been her choice before, but for now, it was exactly the choice she would make. The doorbell rang again.

Sarah put on her robe and looked out the peephole. It was Marcus. She shook her head and started to unlock the door. Changing her mind, she locked it again and opened the window nearest the door.

"Hello, Marcus."

"Will you open the door, Sarah? I want to apologize for last night."

"No, Marcus. You can apologize from there."

"Well, I want to say something more important, too."

"You can say it from there, Marcus."

Marcus turned around. Sarah's condo faced a courtyard with a swimming pool. He turned back with a pleading look on his face. "Please, Sarah."

She had her hand on the door lock, ready to open it. Something inside her said, no, don't unlock that door. Don't unlock it. So she didn't.

"I can hear you fine from here, Marcus. Just talk softly if you don't want anyone else to hear."

He was upset about that; she could tell. Marcus was not a man used to not getting his own way. "Okay!" he said, not in a nice tone. "Sarah, I'm sorry about my, ah, condition last night. I had no right to approach you when I was like that. But I said those words with an open heart. You have always been on my mind, and the only reason I didn't act on that before is because I was married. I may be many things, but I am not a cheater." He

171

waited for a response, but Sarah only nodded.

"So since you said that you had been attracted to me, I wondered if you could maybe find it in your heart to give me a chance. I'll take you out to a nice dinner. We'll have a good time."

"I told you I was in love with someone else, Marcus."

"Oh, I thought you just made that up."

"I said it because it's true."

"Well, if you won't go out with me, would you at least come back to work? I'll give you a substantial raise." Sarah looked at him through the screen. "More vacation." Sarah still stayed silent. "Whatever you want, Sarah. I'll give you whatever you want if you'll come back to work."

"I'm not interested, Marcus. Sorry." She began to close the window, but Marcus held up his hand.

"Wait. I am sorry, and I care for you a great deal."

"Noted," said Sarah. "Good-bye, Marcus. I'm sorry about your divorce." She closed the window and walked away, but she could see in the mirror on her wall that Marcus stayed out there. Walking to a position that she could see him in the mirror, she watched. For more than five minutes, Marcus stood there looking in. She heard him try the door handle, and she was thankful that she had locked it. Then he walked away.

A chill went down her spine and gave her goose bumps. Sarah had known Marcus for more than three years. She had loved him for most of those years. And although she knew that Marcus was not dangerous and not a stalker—the episode made her feel leery. After what happened with Lucius and Sanford, she felt she needed to be more self-protective, more cautious. And yes, more proactive. She knew exactly what she had to do, and she was going to do it right now.

CHAPTER FORTY-FIVE

THE WHOLE TOWN was celebrating. Zack, after Doc bandaged him up, was a hero. Matthew was a hero. Josiah and Nick were heroes. Even Dolly was a hero. At least six or eight times, Matthew had to ask someone to escort Dolly back outside when she had been brought in for a beer or a whiskey. And surprise of all surprises, Rawlins was a hero. Rawlins, pleased with his part in the plan and the honor and respect he received for it, was celebrating the best way he knew how—drinking. Although something had changed. He was drinking sarsaparilla.

With Zack having a difficult time helping with only one hand, Matthew had more work than he could handle. Sometimes Rawlins helped him out. Sometimes another regular. And although Matthew was too busy to have time to think of anything else, every time his gaze fell on the piano, he thought of Sarah. And when she wasn't in his thoughts, it felt like her spirit, or the essence of her, was a constant in his mind behind all the other thoughts. He was filled with longing for her and wondered how soon she would return.

"Congratulations, Matthew! Great job!" Matthew couldn't count how many times he had already heard that. And more and more people kept coming up and congratulating him. So many slaps on the back, and he had downed enough sarsaparilla to suit him for two days.

The other men had received similar accolades—and drinks. Everyone wanted to toast a hero, so all of them received free drinks. Matthew noted that none of them drank much whiskey. Well, Zack drank some—totally unlike him—but it was because his arm still hurt him. And although Josiah had told Nick that he could celebrate if he wanted, Nick declined. So the two of them had one whiskey to every ten sarsaparillas that they drank. Matthew hoped he had enough sarsaparilla to go around. This was an unexpected celebration.

Matthew didn't think there was anyone as happy as he was that the gang was out of the picture. And yet, celebrating over their deaths felt wrong to him somehow. When the door of that cabin opened, and the man with the gun appeared, he had fired along with Josiah and Nick. Zack had been in danger, and Matthew felt that by firing he was protecting him. And when he fired into the window, he was shooting *back* at them. Whether one of his bullets hit anyone, or killed anyone, he would never know. He would prefer not to know.

Matthew did not consider himself a killer. He killed wildlife for him and Zack to eat, and he shot at those men to protect the people he loved—Zack and Sarah. But to celebrate their deaths didn't feel right. He would enjoy the town's celebration; and he would graciously accept the slaps on the back and the drinks offered. But the only thing he wanted to celebrate was that now it was safe for Sarah to return.

Thinking of her made him smile. Matthew longed to see her in his saloon again, playing the piano and singing. Truth was, he would be satisfied just having her back in his life. Sure, he would love to have her in his arms. But if she didn't feel that way about him, then just having her around would be a satisfactory alternative.

"Hallo, Matthew. Where is your mind wandering off to? Aren't you enjoying the celebration?" asked Samuel.

"Sure, it's fine," said Matthew. He liked Samuel. As Matthew had kind of adopted Zack as a brother, Samuel had adopted Matthew and Josiah as sons. His own sons had been reported lost in the Civil War. And Samuel had never been the same after that.

"You didn't tell me about the plan, Matthew. You know I'm a good shot!"

"Aw, Samuel, it was all a secret. I was following instructions from Josiah."

"Josiah is too stingy for his own good. He wants to keep all the fun to himself!"

Samuel was half joking, but Matthew knew that it bothered him. He felt left out. Matthew also knew that Samuel would like to be deputy sheriff, but Josiah wouldn't offer the job to him because Eliza had asked him not to.

"He was afraid that if it accidentally got out, then the plan would fail, and we couldn't catch the other gang members," explained Matthew. "You know, if we hadn't caught them all, Sarah couldn't—or wouldn't—come back."

"So when's she coming?" asked Samuel.

"I don't know," said Matthew, as he smiled at the thought of her return. "I hope soon."

CHAPTER FORTY-SIX

SARAH LOOKED AROUND her condo thinking. It was a mess, with boxes—some full, some sealed, some half-full —strewn all over the place. And although Sarah was a self-proclaimed neat-freak, this didn't bother her. There was a time and place for neatness, and this wasn't the time.

She started sorting the boxes—which ones she needed right away and which ones could go in storage. So far, there was only one box she needed and the rest were for storage. Working quickly, she filled her suitcases with what she thought she'd need. As she packed, she hoped she was packing for her move to the old Red Bluff and not a prolonged stay at Madison's until she found a new place to live in the present Red Bluff.

Sarah hoped that with everything she had in her. Although she didn't know if it would all work out with Matthew, she knew that he was her heart's desire. Because she would also have a singing career in old Red Bluff was another reason to want to return there. But loving Matthew, well, that was number one. Even if she could never sing there again—like if Matthew sold the saloon to some old grouch who didn't want her—she would still want to go there to be with Matthew.

When she thought of Matthew, the word that always came to mind was kind. When she thought of Marcus or even her ex-husband, Carl, the words to describe them would be strong and dynamic. But were they kind? No, not really. Business came first for them, and their women came second. Or came third for Carl. But Matthew was kind, and he treated her kindly. Except when she told him that she had come from the future—and she imagined that would scare anybody—he had always treated her with kindness and respect. She deserved that. Finally. Sarah wasn't sure if she ever thought she deserved that before. But she did, now. And she knew—knew to the depths of her heart—that it was Matthew whom she wanted. It was Matthew whom she loved.

Since she could only bring a minimum amount of belongings back to the old Red Bluff, she finished quickly. Also, she had three bags full of clothes already there. She loaded her car in two quick trips, looked around one last time, and locked the door of her condo. This had been her home for many years. Would she miss it? Once she arrived in the old Red Bluff and settled in to a life of singing and loving Matthew, she didn't think she'd ever give it another thought. It had been comfortable. It had suited her needs. But it was her old life. Now she had a new one, and she was eager to begin it.

Sarah drove over to Madison's—Jenna's old place, really—and parked. Madison wasn't home. When she tried the front door, she found it unlocked, as she expected. The ranch, like so many others out here, was so far out of town that most people left their doors unlocked. A legacy to simpler times.

After unloading her car into the living room, Sarah walked through the hallway to the front of the house. The bedrooms were the same size, but one bedroom had a bigger closet and two windows. That's the one. Sarah brought in her two loads and unpacked them into the dresser and the closet. Then she picked up her smartphone and dialed Gillian's number.

"This is Gillian."

"Hey, Gillian, it's Sarah."

"Hi, Sarah. How's the packing going?"

"That's why I called."

"Oh, do you need more boxes? No problem, I can pick some up and bring them right over, if you want."

"No, no, it's not that. Didn't you say that you had someone who could pack for me?"

"Oh. I had someone who could *help*."

"Let me tell you what I need, Gillian. If you could make it happen, it would be awesome. I just moved out, and I have everything that I need with me. If you could somehow arrange for someone to finish packing up my apartment, and then load it into storage somewhere, I would be very grateful. I'm willing to pay whatever is fair."

"I have some ideas, Sarah. Let me make some calls! Bye!" Gillian hung up the phone. She isn't a person who lets grass grow under her feet, thought Sarah.

Five minutes later, Sarah's phone rang. Sarah recognized the number.

"Hello, Gillian. That was fast," said Sarah.

"If something needs doing, I get 'er done! This is what I have. Two women will come in tomorrow and stay as long as it takes for the packing. When they finish, their husbands will load up all the boxes and take them to a storage unit for you. Do you have a place picked out already, or would you like me to take care of that for you?"

"I would love it if you could take care of that, too, Gillian. And I don't care where it is—there's a good chance I'll never see that stuff again."

"No problem. I'll take care of it. Anything else you need?"

"Oh, yeah. I forgot the wardrobe boxes. Can you—"

"No problem, Sarah. I'll take care of that, too. The other line is ringing. Call me if you need anything else."

"Thanks, Gillian. Let me know how much I owe you. Bye."

"Bye now."

Sarah kicked off her shoes and walked into the living room. She put her feet on the coffee table, put her hands behind her head, and relaxed. Now she didn't have to worry about a return visit from Marcus. He would have no idea where she went. Life was good. After a few more minutes of relaxation, Sarah decided that she would walk out to the barn to see Dancer. Maybe she'd even tell him that they were moving to the old Red Bluff. She thought he'd be pleased about that.

CHAPTER FORTY-SEVEN

WHEN MATTHEW AWOKE, he hoped that it wouldn't be another celebration day. He had enough celebration the day before to last him for a while. A long while. He wanted to relax back into his normal routine. And wait for Sarah to return. Matthew wondered when that would be. How long would it take her to realize the situation with the outlaws was finished? She never needed to be frightened about Lucius or Sanford ever again.

Matthew got up, left his apartment, and walked down the hallway. He knocked on Sarah's door. No answer. Although he realized that it was unlikely that she would have arrived late at night, he didn't want to disturb her accidentally. Opening the door, he peered inside. Just seeing her belongings there gave him some comfort. She had to return. She just had to. There was no reason for her not to—now. The danger was gone.

Before going downstairs, he walked back to the apartment and knocked on Zack's door. He hated to wake him, but he was worried about him. The doctor said that because of the long ride back, he had lost a lot of blood. Luckily, that bandage that Nick had put on his arm had saved him. Doc said it would have been much worse without that.

"Yeah?" asked Zack, sleepily.

Matthew opened the door. "You okay?"

"No, it hurts pretty bad," said Zack.

"Would you like me to bring you breakfast?" asked Matthew.

"No, I'm not hungry. I'll come down later."

"Zack, you don't have to work at all today. Just rest. Come down when you want, and I'll fix you something to eat. But no work for you. Understand?"

"It hurts too much for me to argue," said Zack.

"Hope you feel better, kid," said Matthew, as he closed the door to Zack's room.

Later, after Matthew had eaten and opened the saloon, a few people trickled in. Most of them sat at the poker table, and one or two sat at the bar. But there was no celebration, and for that, Matthew felt grateful.

The rest of the day wasn't too busy, but he was busier than usual because normally Zack brought the drinks to everyone at the tables, and Matthew handled the bar. But now, Matthew had to handle both. It wasn't really taxing, but Matthew would have preferred to relax more. Why did he want to relax? So he could think of Sarah, of course. Until he had her back, he had to be satisfied with just thoughts of her. And as busy as he was that day, he didn't have time to think about her. That made him miss her even more.

It was late afternoon when Josiah and Jenna walked in. They sat at the bar.

"Hi, Matthew," said Josiah, as he looked around. "Where's Zack? He okay?"

"His arm is still hurting," said Matthew.

"Aw, poor kid. I hope he's all right," said Josiah.

"Who's helping you, Matthew?" asked Jenna.

Matthew smiled. "I'm doing it all!"

Jenna stood up from the bar and walked to the poker table. She had noticed the men there were waving their hands.

"When's Sarah coming back, Matthew?" asked Josiah.

"I don't know," said Matthew. "I hope soon."

"When did you tell her?" asked Josiah.

Before Matthew could answer, Jenna walked back to the bar. "Two whiskeys and a beer."

Matthew put them on a tray, handed them to her, and said, "Thank you.

"*I* haven't told her," said Matthew to Josiah. "I'm not going to the *future*," he whispered.

"Sakes alive, Matthew! There are some cool things there!" said Josiah.

"Cool? What do you mean?"

"Oh, sorry. I'm starting to talk like Jenna! Some neat new inventions. You oughta see cars and trucks! To ride in a car is rip roaring fun! I'm trying to talk Jenna into teaching me to drive! But you have to try the Thai restaurant that we go to. Delicious! Really!"

"Josiah!" called Rawlins from a side table.

"Be right back," said Josiah, as he stood up and walked to see Rawlins.

Jenna sat down when he left. "Everybody's taken care of for now, Matthew."

"Thanks, Jenna. I appreciate that."

"So when's Sarah coming back?"

"I don't know. Hopefully soon."

"Who told her?" asked Jenna.

"No one that I know of," said Matthew. "I thought

she'd—you know—*know*."

"Why? Because," she lowered her voice, "she's from the future? We can't read minds, Matthew! We're like everybody else. Would you like me to take you to her? That way you could tell her yourself."

"No, Jenna, no, I have no desire to go to the future. Despite the 'cool' cars and trucks and the tiger restaurant."

Jenna laughed. "Ah, you've been talking to Josiah! Tiger restaurant? What's that?"

"He said that you go there, and it's delicious."

"Oh! The Thai restaurant! Yes, it is wonderful. Come on, Matthew, give it a shot. Sarah would appreciate it if you go get her yourself."

"I can honestly say, Jenna, that I will never go to the future. It's just not me."

"Even if there was no way for Sarah to find out that it's safe here?"

Matthew moved his head from side to side. "That's not a fair question, because I know that Nick is going back in a week. I hate to wait that long, but I know he *is* going back. But to answer your question, no, I can't do it. Sarah will have to come here. To me."

"Oh, Matthew! I'd be happy to take you. Or Josiah could, too, if you'd be more comfortable with him. He knows the way."

"It's not that, Jenna. I just want to stay in town. Right here."

"Okay, if you feel that way. But you'd see her that much sooner if you go yourself."

Matthew shook his head and began pouring drinks for two men at the other end of the bar. He missed Sarah, a lot, but he wouldn't—no, he *couldn't* go to the future to see her.

Josiah walked up and put his arm around Jenna. "You ready, Sweetie?"

"Sure am!" She stood up and kissed him on his lips. "Matthew, if you change your mind, Josiah and I are available." Then she turned, and she and Josiah walked out through the swinging doors together.

CHAPTER FORTY-EIGHT

AFTER LEAVING MADISON a note, Sarah had gone to sleep early the night before. She slept well, but woke up disoriented. It took her awhile to figure out where she was. First she thought she was in the old Red Bluff, and then she saw the electric clock on the dresser.

Sarah lay in bed a long time wondering about what had happened with the outlaws. Was Matthew hurt? Was that why she hadn't heard from him? Were the outlaws so far away that they were still chasing them? Or did they give up and Matthew didn't have the heart to tell her? All valid questions, and no way to get an answer until someone came to the future to tell her. Or she went back there—and that wasn't going to happen—at least not until she knew it was safe.

She thought back on the events that had happened to her. Although it was only a week ago, it already felt surreal, as if it had happened to someone else, or as if she had seen it in a movie. Was she really almost raped and killed? Did they really rescue her just in time? Did it all really happen? Was Matthew real? Was the cave that led to 1870 real?

186

So much had happened in the last week, starting with her kidnapping, through selling her condo and quitting her job, and ending with Marcus declaring his love for her. It was all too much. Sarah just wanted to hide.

Living at Jenna's ranch with Madison was already like hiding. Sarah stretched and forced herself out of bed. Time to start the day! If she couldn't hide, then she would do the next best thing: ride. She dressed and walked out to the barn. Dancer nickered when he saw her.

"Hi, Dancer. What a good boy you are!" Sarah stroked the side of his head and ran her hand down his neck along his mane. "Would you like to go for a ride today?"

In answer, the horse nuzzled her. Sarah saddled and bridled him, walked him out to the paddock, and climbed on. "Let's go, boy." When they arrived at the main trail, Sarah didn't have the heart to turn right toward the cave, so she guided the horse to her left.

After an hour of riding, Sarah felt better. She felt as if her head had cleared. Unfortunately, the situation in the old Red Bluff came clear to her as well. Obviously something had gone wrong. And the longer it took anyone to tell her about it, the worse it was. Maybe Matthew was even dead. Maybe he had been killed while trying to get the outlaws.

What if she had finally found her own true love—Matthew—and now he was dead? What would she do then? Would she even return to the old Red Bluff? She had to find out. Even if it was bad news, she wanted to know. Sometimes the unknown was much worse than knowing something bad.

She turned Dancer around and headed back toward

the ranch. When they passed it, she gave Dancer his head and let him run. Toward the cave. Toward her love. Sarah slowed him down before the turnoff, and they headed up the steep trail at a walk.

Maybe she could go back there herself. Even if they hadn't caught the outlaws, they wouldn't be so stupid to hang out around Red Bluff. Would they? But she had to find out! She couldn't wait a moment more without knowing. It had to be now.

Dancer turned off toward the cave without being asked. He had come here often enough. When they got to the mouth of the cave, Sarah reined him in. She looked into the depths of the cave and realized that she couldn't do it. Tears fell silently down her face. Dancer stamped his foot, impatient to go on. Sarah patted his neck to calm him down. Not that Dancer was ever a calm horse, but it might settle him a little. Finally, in a fit of anguish over the injustice of it all, angry with the outlaws for making her feel this way, and angry with herself for not having the courage to return to Red Bluff, she screamed into the cave.

"Matthew! Matthew!" She screamed it over and over and over again. Although she knew he couldn't hear her, she hoped that somehow he would get the message. She wanted him to know how important he was to her, how much she loved him, and how she would do anything for him, but she couldn't return to Red Bluff until she knew what had happened.

Sarah, her voice raw from screaming, her face red from crying, returned to the ranch feeling like a failure. After unsaddling and brushing Dancer, she walked back to the house. Madison was gone again, and had left her a note that said she'd be back later. That was fine. Sarah didn't feel like she was up to visiting with anyone, anyway. She flopped onto her bed and cried herself to sleep.

CHAPTER FORTY-NINE

WHEN MATTHEW WOKE up, he immediately sighed. Sarah still wasn't back. And although Nick was going back in less than a week, Matthew had still not even asked him to tell Sarah. From what he understood, the new Red Bluff was much bigger than the old Red Bluff, so there was no guarantee that he'd even see her—unless Matthew asked him to.

Could he wait that long to see her? What were his choices? Matthew couldn't go to the future, that much was certain. His life was here, with or without Sarah. He hoped it was with Sarah. His reluctance to go to the future had no relationship to how he felt about her. He loved her madly. She occupied all his thoughts. She was the most important person in his life. He would do anything for her—except go to the future.

A sound from the other room disturbed Matthew's thoughts. Zack! He was important to Matthew, too. What was that sound? Matthew jumped out of bed and knocked on Zack's door.

"You okay in there? Need any help?"

Zack opened the door and looked at Matthew through

bloodshot eyes. "I'm doing better today, Matthew. It still hurts, but not as much. Josiah said it would ache for a few days. I can work today. Were you too busy yesterday? I'm sorry I couldn't help."

"No problem at all, Zack. Jenna helped for a while, and later even Rawlins helped! What a surprise that was —to everyone in the saloon! He's been sober for days now.

"You can stay in bed if you need to, Zack. I don't want you to work if you're not feeling good." Matthew knew that Zack was a hard worker and liked doing his share. But he didn't want him to work too soon and risk damaging his arm any further.

"No, Matthew, really. I'm feeling much better today. I want to work."

"Okay, how about I fix us some breakfast?"

"Sounds great, Matthew. Thanks."

As they were eating breakfast, Zack asked, "When is Sarah coming back?"

Matthew shook his head. "I don't know."

"You mean you haven't told her yet that the scalawags are all dead?"

"No, Zack, I haven't. I can't go to where she is right now."

"Why not? *I* can! I'll tell her for you!"

"Zack, you can't even ride a horse with your arm hurting like that. Thanks, but no."

"Well, who's going to tell her?"

"I don't know, Zack. Nick is going back there in a few days. But I haven't asked him to tell her. Yet."

"Why not, Matthew? We *need* Sarah here. Her smile lights up the place. You know that people come here to hear her sing. She's good for business! We have to get her back."

Matthew sighed and looked at his eggs. "She's good for a lot more than that."

Zack laughed. "Yes, Matthew, and because you love her!"

Matthew looked up suddenly. "How do *you* know?"

"Don't you remember? You told me! But even if you hadn't, I would have known because whenever she's around, you have that moony look on your face. It's pretty obvious."

"You smart aleck, kid! You're too smart for your own good! I'm going to have to take those books away from you!" Matthew put his hand in a fist and moved it toward Zack's shoulder, until he realized that was his sore arm. "Enough about Sarah. She's my problem, and I'll deal with it. If it's meant to happen, it will, and I'm not going to push it."

"She's not yours yet, Matthew," Zack said seriously. "She's my friend, too, and I want her here. When are you going to ask Nick to talk to her?"

"I don't know. Listen, I'll load up the bar, and you can relax until we open," Matthew said, trying to change the subject.

Zack stood up. "*I'm* going to go ask Nick right now." Before Matthew could protest, Zack marched from the room and out the front door.

CHAPTER FIFTY

WHEN SARAH AWOKE later in the afternoon, she found another note from Madison. It said she had left again and wouldn't be back until late, but she hoped they could connect the following day.

Sarah made a quick trip to the grocery store for some food and snacks, came home, and ate blue tortilla chips with guacamole dip. After stuffing herself with that, she walked back to her bedroom and turned on the television to see if it worked. It did. She wasn't a big television watcher, but she did enjoy it occasionally. Could she give it up completely? No doubt about the answer to that one, a big yes. No biggie.

Sarah clicked through the channels until she found an old western that she had watched years earlier. Back then she thought that it seemed realistic. Now, after spending so much time in the old Red Bluff, she laughed at how far off they were from the truth. After watching for fifteen minutes, she clicked through to the weather channel. The western made her long for the past, long for Matthew.

She fell asleep to the descriptions of a storm front

hitting the east coast. Although she slept fitfully through the night, she didn't get up until morning. Sarah stretched and thought that maybe this would be the day that *someone* would tell her the outcome of what happened with the outlaws. The not knowing was killing her. And the longer it took, the more she thought that maybe something had gone wrong—maybe even terribly wrong.

She fixed herself some eggs and coffee for breakfast—which of course reminded her of eating breakfast at the Red Bluff hotel. "Please, not another reminder of the old Red Bluff. I can't take it."

"What'd ya say, Sarah?" asked Madison, as she bounced into the room.

"Oh, I didn't know you were awake yet. I was just talking to myself," said Sarah.

"You want to go running with me this morning? It will make you feel better," said Madison.

"No, thanks. I'm more of a sitter than a runner."

Madison opened the front door, and while she was running in place, said over her shoulder, "Sarah, maybe we could go riding when I return." Without waiting for an answer, she slid through the door, closed it, and disappeared.

Sarah spent the next hour going over various scenarios in her mind of horrible things that might have happened when they went after the outlaws. All of them included something bad happening to Matthew. Some of them included something bad happening to Nick or Zack. None of them included anything bad happening to Josiah. Before Jenna got involved with him, she had searched genealogy sites on the internet and discovered that he didn't die for many, many years. Although, he still might have gotten hurt. Maybe that's why Jenna hasn't come to tell her—she's taking care of a hurt Josiah. Sarah sighed. The thoughts in her mind were ridiculous, and she was just making herself miserable.

Madison rushed into the house. Not even out of breath after an hour run. Wow, thought Sarah, I'm impressed.

"You ready to go for a ride?" asked Madison.

"Don't you need to rest or anything?"

"No, I'm good. Just let me change clothes and put my boots on. I'll be ready in a couple of minutes."

By the time Sarah had put her own boots on and combed her hair, Madison was ready. They walked out to the barn and brushed and saddled their horses. Then they were off. When they reached the main trail, Madison wanted to go right, toward the cave.

"Madison, I don't have the heart to go that way. Let's go left, instead."

"Tell me what's going on, Sarah. Ryan told me what happened and about some plan to catch the hoodlums that did that to you. But I don't know anything since. Did they catch the bad guys?"

"I don't know. I wish I knew."

"What do you mean you don't know? No one came to tell you? Or you didn't go back to find out?"

"I can't go back, Madison. You can't imagine how terrifying that experience was. I'm still not over it. There is no way I can return until I know they are locked away. And hopefully the key is thrown away."

"And no one has come to tell you what happened?"

"No, and it's scaring me more and more. I'm so afraid that something awful has happened, and that's why no one has told me."

"Oh, don't think that way, Sarah. There could be

many reasons no one has come to tell you."

"Like what?" asked Sarah.

"I don't know! Lots of reasons! I wouldn't worry about it, if I were you."

"I wish I could stop worrying about it."

"Why don't you just get the bad things that happened to you out of your head, and just go over there. Even if they never caught the bad guys, they wouldn't be stupid enough to hang around Red Bluff anymore."

"I can't do it, Madison, I just can't do it. Until I find out what happened, I'm stuck here."

"Oh, Sarah, just do it!"

"I can't." Sarah hesitated. "But you can! You could go there for me and find out! And come right back!" Sarah looked around. They were riding on a trail that she wasn't familiar with. They had twisted and turned, and seemed to be going in a different direction now.

"I wish I could, Sarah, but I have homework to complete tonight and an early class tomorrow morning. Finals are coming up. I'll be busy all week. Sorry."

"Oh, that's all right. It was a long shot, anyway."

"If nobody comes by next weekend, then I can probably go. You should have asked yesterday. Then it would have worked out. Sorry."

Why didn't I ask yesterday, Sarah wondered. Because all she could think about was someone coming to tell her. She didn't consider the possibility of someone going there to find out. Now it was too late.

Madison had turned her horse left up a steep bank that felt vaguely familiar to Sarah. Dancer followed Madison's horse. A few minutes later, Madison stopped and said, "Here we are! Now's your chance, Sarah. Go for it!"

Sarah looked up and saw the mouth of the cave. Her mouth dropped open with surprise. Madison had taken her some roundabout way and come at the steep turnoff from the opposite direction. The little trickster!

"No, Madison, I can't."

"Yes you can! Of course you can! Just do it! Once you get over there, you'll be fine."

"I can't, Madison, but you can."

"It's too late for me, Sarah. I need to get back before dark—and in time to study. But since you're not coming back, you could do this! I know you can."

Tears began to roll down Sarah's face. "I can't. I just can't."

Madison turned when she heard the quiver in Sarah's voice and noticed the tears. "I'm sorry, Sarah. Let's go back now. I'm sorry." She turned her horse and walked past Dancer. Sarah moved the reins, and Dancer followed Madison's horse all the way back to the ranch.

CHAPTER FIFTY-ONE

AT FIRST, MATTHEW felt huffed at what Zack was about to do. But it passed quickly. And besides, Matthew knew that he wasn't the kind of guy who made things happen, so it was just as well that Zack would do it for him. He hoped that was okay with Sarah. It had to be. Matthew couldn't change the way he was.

As the annoyance left, Matthew was left with a quiet joy. Sarah would be here soon. His beautiful, wonderful Sarah would be here. With him. Unless—what if she *would* be angry with him for not coming to get her himself? She would just have to understand. He couldn't go to the future. He just couldn't. And he hoped that she would understand.

Matthew didn't know what took Zack so long. It was less than a minute walk to the sheriff's office to see Nick. Maybe he wasn't there, and Zack had to go find him someplace. Part of him wished that Zack would leave it alone. But the rest of him felt glad that Zack was willing to talk to Nick.

It wasn't that Matthew was afraid to talk to Nick. Matthew could talk to anyone—that wasn't the problem.

What bothered Matthew was that it was somewhere between not wanting to ask for a favor and wanting to let everything turn out the way it would.

Eventually, Sarah would somehow learn of the outlaws' demise. If not from Nick, then from Ryan or Jenna. Or some other person from the future would have come here, found out, and brought the information back to Sarah. That woman that Zack liked—oh yeah, Madison. And her mother, Kat. Someone would tell Sarah.

So by not asking Nick, it wasn't that Matthew was giving up on her. He was just letting it happen when it was meant to happen. Now he wondered if by Zack forcing the issue, it would change the way everything turned out. It didn't matter. The sooner he got his Sarah back, the better.

As Matthew was stocking the whiskey, Zack returned. Matthew looked up and saw Zack walking toward him, all smiles.

"What?" asked Matthew.

"I did it. I took care of it."

Matthew looked down at what he was doing. "Well, then. Okay. Thank you."

"The latest Sarah will find out is this weekend, when Nick goes back."

"What do you mean 'the latest'?"

"After I talked to Nick, I walked over to the store and talked to Ryan. He said he wasn't planning to return any time soon, but in case he did, he would be happy to report to Sarah the coast is clear, whatever that means."

"Nick would have been enough," said Matthew.

"Maybe, but I didn't stop at Ryan, either," said Zack with a smile. "Then I walked over to the school, to talk to that new schoolteacher, Rachel. She said there was a chance she would return Friday after school, but if not, it wouldn't be until next week. But if she did return Friday, she would definitely tell Sarah that she could safely return." Zack smiled at Matthew and looked completely pleased with himself.

"I was going to talk to Granny, too, but Ryan said that she hadn't returned once since she moved here, and he didn't think she had any plans of ever returning," said Zack. "Where are they all from, Matthew? Do you know? It's a mystery. No one will talk about it."

"Someplace I've never been, Zack," said Matthew, truthfully. "Anyway, thank you for taking the time to talk to everyone. It's not something I would have done, but I'm glad it's done. So, thank you.

"By the way, how's your arm?" asked Matthew.

"Feeling better. The pain isn't too bad now. I can work today, no problem."

The rest of the day, Matthew had a slight smile on his face anticipating Sarah's arrival. He didn't know how soon she would arrive, but she was coming home. She was coming home.

CHAPTER FIFTY-TWO

MATTHEW THOUGHT ABOUT what Zack had said, "this weekend." What did that mean? The previous evening, Friday, he thought maybe Nick would stop by, but he didn't. After waiting all week and still no Sarah, Matthew hoped he didn't have to wait until Sunday. Although, what's one more day after waiting this long? One more day was one day too many.

And once Nick told her, how soon would she be here? The same day? The following day? What if she wasn't ready? What if she had decided it was too dangerous here—whether the outlaws were caught or not—and had decided against coming back altogether? What would he do then?

He wished that Sarah didn't come from the future. That made everything so much more complicated. It would be so much easier if she was just from another nearby town. Matthew considered himself just a country boy, and being in love with someone from the future was a stretch. And yet, it was too late for him now. Once he had given his heart, he couldn't get it back. He knew that for sure.

It had been a busy morning and afternoon, so Matthew was busy restocking the bar. And he didn't recognize the voice when it ordered a beer, so he didn't get excited until he turned around and saw Nick standing there.

"Nick!" exclaimed Matthew, in surprise. When Nick nodded, Matthew tried to hide his excitement. "You drinkin' on the job, now?"

"Nope. I'm off now. About to go back home."

Matthew gave him a beer and waited for Nick to say something about Sarah.

"Zack already asked me to tell Sarah about our success, but I was wondering if you had any personal message for her," said Nick.

"Ah, well, yeah, I guess. Could you, um, just tell her that I love her? And I'm hoping that she comes home soon. I wouldn't know what else to say. I really miss her."

Nick smiled and took another sip of beer. "I'm sure she'll be happy to hear that, Matthew."

"How soon do you think you'll see her?"

"Well, if she's at Jenna's ranch like Ryan thinks she is, then it will be about an hour after I leave here. A lot less if I give my horse his head."

Matthew nodded and, when the words sunk in, said, "Sarah is less than an hour from here?"

"That's right. I'd be happy to take you there, Matthew. You'd see her that much sooner."

"Oh, no, no, I can't do that."

"There's nothing to be afraid of, honest. Besides some major differences," Nick laughed, "it's pretty much the same."

"It's not that I'm afraid," said Matthew.

"What is it, then?" asked Nick.

"I'm just a country boy."

"So?"

"I'm just a country boy," Matthew lowered his voice, "and I don't belong in the future."

"Matthew, if you think like that, then maybe Sarah doesn't belong in the past."

Matthew looked up quickly to see that Nick looked at him seriously. Not knowing what else to do, Matthew shrugged.

"Matthew, Jenna is from there, and she married Josiah. You can see how happy they are. Granny is from there, and she married Edward. You can see they are both still old grouches!" Nick laughed. "Ryan is from there and loves it here. Rachel, your new schoolteacher, is from there. I just made an arrangement with Josiah, and I will be here every third weekend. We're all from there, but we love it here. It's not unnatural or anything."

"But nobody from here has gone there to live," said Matthew.

"That's because it's so much nicer here! But almost everyone has returned there and will keep returning, periodically. Most of us still have ties there, reasons to go back. If you go there to see Sarah, you don't have to stay. Just bring her back with you! She'd love it if you went to get her." Nick leaned forward conspiratorially. "Women like that kind of thing, you know."

Matthew turned away while Nick finished his beer. He wished he was the kind of man who could just pick up and go out to find Sarah. But he wasn't. And he was okay with that. He wasn't going to push himself beyond his limits. That wouldn't be good for him, and it wouldn't be good for Sarah. He turned back to Nick.

"Thanks for everything, Nick. I appreciate you telling

Sarah that I love her. But I can't go back there. I just can't."

"Okay, I'll tell her, and hopefully you'll see her soon." Nick stood up to leave.

"Nick." Matthew fished in his pocket and looked at the coins. He picked out a gold one, kissed it, and handed it to Nick. "Give her this for me, will you? She likes gold coins."

Nick nodded and walked out of the saloon. Matthew turned toward the back of the bar and wiped a tear from his eye. He hoped to see Sarah soon.

CHAPTER FIFTY-THREE

SARAH FELT DISAPPOINTED that Madison couldn't go to the old Red Bluff for her. She understood, but she still felt disappointed. It would have been perfect—she could've gone there and back in one day. And Sarah would know. She would know that she could return there and feel safe.

How she longed to feel safe again. It wasn't just that she missed her singing and missed Matthew. It was that she wanted to feel safe. And she knew that she couldn't feel safe until someone told her that those outlaws had been caught. She felt a chill go through her body. A horrible thought. They could potentially come here. There's no reason to think that those outlaws couldn't stumble onto the cave and come here. And find her.

Maybe it wasn't such a good idea that she moved from her condo to the ranch. They never could have found her at her condo. But here, at the ranch, she was just off the main trail. The chill came again, and she fought it off. No! That's a stupid thought! They are far away from either Red Bluff—the old one and the new one. Even if they weren't caught, they weren't close to anywhere that mattered.

Setting her irrational fears of the outlaws coming to the new Red Bluff aside, what bothered her most was not knowing if Matthew was okay or not. Surely if something terrible had happened to him, *someone* would have come back and told her. Wouldn't they?

She sighed and looked out the window as the sky was darkening. Another day gone by, and no news. Well, her mother used to tell her, "no news is good news." She'd have to hope that was true. Because right now, no news was the only news that she had.

The following days were a mix of hope, disappointment, and boredom. A time or two, the thought crossed her mind that maybe she shouldn't have paid someone to pack her house. It would have at least given her something to do. On the other hand, she was grateful to be out of there. Marcus had called exactly seventeen times since she saw him at her condo. Seventeen times, and Sarah didn't return any of the calls.

After that first time, she never allowed herself to fantasize on how it might feel being married to Marcus. That was who she was before. It was not who she was now. She was a different person now, a different Sarah. And the new Sarah was in love with Matthew, who was *nothing* like Marcus. And she was grateful for that.

Sarah spent the next few days taking long horseback rides just to have something to do. Although she stayed away from the trail to the cave, one day she did try to recreate the path where Madison had taken her. But she found herself hopelessly lost and had to depend on Dancer to find his way home. Luckily, he did.

Sarah didn't know what day Nick would return. She knew he had to be back at work by Monday at the latest.

So, would he come back Friday night, Saturday, Sunday? There was no way to know. But it would be soon. She knew that. And just in case he was in a hurry and didn't think to tell her what had happened, she had put a big note on his truck. He couldn't miss it.

Thursday, Madison offered to ride out there after school Friday and return Saturday with the news. But Sarah told her that Nick had to be back this weekend. A day or two more wouldn't make that much difference. It was actually killing her, but after waiting this long, she could wait.

Friday night came and went. When Sarah woke up Saturday morning, she immediately looked out the window to see if Nick's truck was still there. It was. She dressed, ate breakfast, and started cleaning house. That often settled her. Madison kept a clean house, but it could always use a little more cleaning. Besides, she was so nervous that cleaning was all she could concentrate on.

It had been a long morning of cleaning and re-cleaning. She had vacuumed the carpet in the living room at least three times. Before Madison left to go hiking, she had finally asked Sarah to stop. So now the sinks were all shiny clean and bright. Even shinier than they were after the *second* time she cleaned them. But instead of cleaning them a fourth time, she finally sat on the couch and waited. And waited and waited.

When she was about to give up hope that Nick would return Saturday, she heard a knock at the door.

CHAPTER FIFTY-FOUR

WHEN SARAH HAD imagined this moment, she thought that she would run as fast as she could to the front door. Instead, as she moved in that direction, it felt as if she were moving in slow motion. Either that, or the door kept moving farther away from her. Finally, after what felt like way too long, she had her hand on the doorknob.

"Nick!" She said his name before the door was all the way open.

"Easy, Sarah girl, easy. Your boy is all right. And he wanted me to tell you that he loves you and misses you."

"Good," said Sarah. "Good. What about the outlaws? Did you catch them?"

"Well, not exactly caught them."

"Oh," sighed Sarah, disappointed.

"We caught up with them, and after a shoot-out, they were all, uh, taken care of."

"Oh, I thought you would take them prisoner or something."

"It doesn't always work out the way that you want it to."

"Was anyone other than the outlaws hurt?"

"Zack got shot in the arm, but he's okay."

"Oh, good. Glad he's okay," said Sarah. "Ryan told me there was a plan, but he didn't tell me what it was. You have time to tell me now?"

"Sure, Sarah, just let me put my horse up. I knew you'd want to know right away."

"Thanks so much for that, Nick. Hey, you want some coffee?"

"That would be awesome. See you in a few."

Sarah watched him walk out to his horse, then she closed the door and made coffee. Before Nick returned to the house, she just wanted to luxuriate in the freedom of knowing that Matthew was okay. And that she didn't have to worry about the outlaws anymore—either finding their way to the future or returning to the old Red Bluff.

She felt bad they were dead. That's never what she intended for them, even though they had intended to kill her. Although back in those days, they probably would have been hanged anyway. Still, she hated that they had to die. Somehow, she felt responsible. A shoot-out. Luckily, Zack had not been badly hurt. Those outlaws might have killed one of the good guys. And it might have been Matthew.

Tears came to her eyes. She wanted to breathe through them, but they just kept coming. Tears of relief swept over her until her whole body was racked with sobs. She couldn't stop.

Nick came through the door, sat down on the couch beside her, and put his arms around her. "It's okay, Sarah. He's okay. Everyone is okay, and the outlaws were dealt with. No worries."

Madison came through the front door. When she saw

Nick embracing Sarah, she said, "Oh, Matthew!"

Nick picked up his head so she could see. "No, Madison, it's just me."

"Oh, it's you," she said with sudden distaste. "You better leave Sarah alone or Matthew will kick your butt."

"It's okay, Madison," said Sarah. "He was comforting me while I was crying tears of relief. Matthew is okay. Everyone is okay. Well, except Zack. He got shot in the arm."

That caught Madison's interest. "Zack? Is he okay? Should we bring him here to the hospital? Should I go there and take care of him?"

"Chill, Madison," said Nick. "He'll be fine. Doc fixed him up, and he's recovering. No worries."

"Oh, okay. As long as he's okay," said Madison. "Well, Sarah, glad Matthew's okay. Did they get the outlaws?"

"Yes, we got them," said Nick.

"Great. Sarah, you can go back now! You don't have to worry about them coming back for you!"

Sarah nodded. "Finally. I know Matthew's safe, and I know I'll be safe." She exhaled slowly, closing her eyes.

"Well, talk to you later," Madison said, as she walked in the back toward her bedroom.

"Nick, tell me the plan. I'm interested in how it all worked."

"Josiah got the idea as we put Sanford in the cell next to Rawlins—you know how Rawlins has been sleeping in an empty cell, right?" Without waiting for an answer, Nick went on. "Josiah made a big deal of searching Rawlins and pretending that he sometimes went in there with the keys to the cells on him. And although it looks like the plan depended on Rawlins, we could have arranged it even if he couldn't handle his part. But he did."

"What do you mean?"

"Rawlins has been on the wagon since the day we brought Sanford in!"

"You're kidding!"

"No, and he still is! He still goes to the saloon every day, but he drinks sarsaparilla, now. The transformation has been remarkable. He was even saluted as a hero after everything was over!"

"Wow."

"Anyway, Josiah had Matthew come in and ask about when the judge was coming and then act indignant with Sanford. The indignant part was a no-brainer. Matthew was furious about what had happened. I just made sure that Sanford heard the judge was coming Saturday.

"Friday night, Rawlins pretended he was drunk, grabbed the keys, and pretended to fall asleep right next to Sanford's cell. I had been practicing fake snoring all week, so I was at my desk pretending I was asleep.

"After some difficulty, thanks to Rawlins's excellent performance, Sanford 'managed' to get the keys from him and unlock his cell. This was all arranged deliberately to happen after the saloon closed. So Sanford crept out the door and noticed a horse tied in front of the saloon. It was Dolly, Jenna's mare, who we had put there for him."

"I know Dolly! You did that because she's so slow!"

"Yes, exactly. Then we had Matthew, Josiah, and lastly Zack planted on the road at intervals. Zack at the end. Zack was to follow Sanford after he went by, by using his tracking skills, and leave little stones on the path so the rest of us wouldn't lose the trail." Nick told her the rest of the story in detail, including how Zack got shot (but was okay), and how Sanford almost took Zack as a hostage.

"Wow! What a story! It sounds like something out of a western movie."

"That's exactly what it was like! We should have filmed it!" Nick laughed.

"Thanks for the details, Nick. And the message from Matthew. I appreciate it."

"No problem, Sarah." He stood up and walked toward the door. "Oh, I almost forgot." Nick stuck his hand in his pocket and flipped the coin to Sarah. "Matthew asked me to give you this."

Sarah caught the coin and held it to her heart. "Thanks, Nick!"

After the front door closed, as Madison walked from her bedroom, she asked, "Is *he* gone?"

"Yeah. Why don't you like him? He told me all about Matthew and the outlaws."

"He's a jerk!"

"Why do you say that? He isn't my type of guy, but he's always been nice to me."

"Well, my mom had a crush on him for years. And he was always a jerk about it. I think she's over him now, though."

"I think he's all right. He just did me a huge favor, and I appreciate it."

"So when are you going back? Do you want me to help carry your bags out so you can leave right away?"

"It's almost dark, Madison. It's too late today."

"So, tomorrow, then?"

Sarah shook her head and shrugged her shoulders. "I don't know. I've been so worried about Matthew and so afraid to go back, that I almost want to sit with it for a day or two. Get used to feeling okay again."

"I thought you were so eager to go back?"

"I am. And now I'm free to go anytime."

"Okay. I don't understand, but okay. If you want me to help you with anything, just let me know."

"Thanks, Madison. I appreciate it."

CHAPTER FIFTY-FIVE

SARAH SAT ON the couch with the gold coin held to her heart for a long time. At times, she just sat there and smiled. Matthew knew that she liked gold coins (although he didn't know why), and he had sent one along to her. That was so sweet! She sighed and pressed the coin into her heart. At other times, she closed her eyes and thought about what life was going to feel like in the old Red Bluff—wondering what it would feel like to live there. Jenna didn't have any complaints. Although she was madly in love with Josiah, which made any minor inconveniences of the times insignificant. Am I madly in love with Matthew, Sarah wondered. The answer came quickly. Oh yeah, madly, completely in love. No doubts.

She felt such a sense of peace and relief, and it felt so good, that it immobilized her. All she could do was sit on the couch, clutching the coin. That's all she wanted to do. The relief of knowing that she didn't have to be afraid anymore and that Matthew was safe, felt so good after all those days of worry that she didn't want to *do* anything about it. She just wanted to feel it. So she spent the rest of the evening doing just that.

Sarah fell asleep that night with a smile on her lips and awoke the same way. Immediately, she searched for the coin that she had left on the nightstand beside the bed. Then she kissed it. She bet herself that Matthew had kissed it before giving it to Nick. It was a silly thought, she knew, but that's what she would keep in her heart. Did Matthew love her enough to look silly in front of another man? Of course he did.

After getting dressed and eating a quick breakfast, Sarah returned to her room to pack. Because she hadn't known how long she'd be staying at the ranch, she had unpacked everything into the closet and dresser. But before she began, a thought crossed her mind. Toilet paper! Matthew had gotten her the composting toilet, but the catalog beside it just wouldn't do. Some modern conveniences she just couldn't do without! Since she didn't know when she would return to the new Red Bluff, she needed toilet paper, and a lot of it.

The checker at the store thought she was crazy for buying all that toilet paper, but Sarah didn't care. After loading it into her car, Sarah stepped in, and her smartphone rang. It was Gillian.

"Hey, Sarah, just wanted to let you know that those people finished packing your condo. They cleaned it out, cleaned it up, and delivered everything safe into storage."

"Thank you so much, Gillian, for taking care of that for me."

"No problem. I was happy to do it. Listen, since you talked about leaving, I wanted to remind you that you have to be here for closing."

"Oh! I completely forgot! I'm glad you mentioned it. When is it?"

"In three weeks." Gillian gave her the exact date, and

Sarah dutifully wrote it down. Then they said their good-byes, and Sarah headed for home.

As Sarah was unloading her car, Madison returned from her morning run. "What's all this for?"

"I can give up my smartphone, but there are some things that I can't give up. Toilet paper is one of them!"

Madison laughed. "I get it, I get it. How are you going to get all this back there?"

"Pack it tightly! And leave some here. I'm going to have to leave some of my belongings behind, also, is that okay Madison?"

"Sure, no problem. I still have another spare bedroom in case anyone wants to stay over."

Madison helped Sarah bring everything into the house, and the women dropped their armloads onto the bed. "It's funny," said Madison. "I never thought of toilet paper as a modern convenience."

"You've stayed there—those catalogs get a little scratchy, don't you think?"

"Yes, definitely! Do you think you're going to leave today?"

"As eager as I am to get there, I don't want to rush and leave something important behind. So I'm going to relax, take my time, and if I finish with time to spare, I'll ride over today. Otherwise, or even if I feel too tired, I'll wait for tomorrow. I want to be at my best when I arrive."

"I understand. I'll leave you to your packing now. Good luck!"

Madison left the room, and Sarah went right to work. She pulled the two empty bags from the closet. Since she knew she had to return in three weeks to sign over her condo, she didn't need to bring as much toilet paper as she had anticipated. So she had more room left over to bring more clothes. That worked out perfectly, she thought.

Sarah filled one bag almost to the top with toilet paper, which she had to squish to get it all in. But squished toilet paper still worked better than catalogs— and felt better, too. The small amount of space left over in that bag, she filled with underthings.

Her second bag proved more of a problem. As she was about to begin, she realized that she had to return to the store. She had decided that she was not yet prepared to give up her smartphone. It may not be too "smart" in the old Red Bluff, and she realized that she couldn't get calls there, but still she wanted it with her. So she drove back to the store and picked up a solar cell phone charger. While she was there, she looked and looked and finally found another solar device that Jenna had to charge various objects. That one she would probably leave behind until her next visit back to the present. After three weeks, she would no doubt have some modern electrical appliances that she missed.

Back at the ranch house, Sarah again tried to fill the second bag. After packing and repacking several times, she realized that she wasn't going to make the trip before dark. Deciding which of her favorite clothes to leave behind was more of a chore than she had anticipated. Finally, after rearranging everything several times, she laid all her clothes out on the bed. Then she separated them into must haves, want but don't need, and her last pile reluctantly labeled "leave behind." In her mind, though, she added "for now" to that label. When she had packed the last item and put the rest away, it was fully dark. And Sarah felt exhausted. But she was also ready for a new day—and her new life.

CHAPTER FIFTY-SIX

MATTHEW THOUGHT FOR sure that Sarah would ride over as soon as she found out all was safe. It was probably too late when Nick told her, but surely Matthew expected her to show up the following day. And here it was the end of that day, and still no Sarah. Why? Did she decide not to come back at all? Was she still too afraid to return? What else could it be?

So many people had asked about Sarah since she had gone. She had made many friends in a short time, and everyone felt her absence. Although no one missed her as much as he did. Of that he was sure. Matthew didn't think that a minute had gone by since her retreat, that he had not thought about her. Sarah was always on his mind. Always. He wondered if she could feel it—feel it through the time, through the century that separated them. He hoped so.

Then a cold thought tore at his heart. What if she didn't take the gold coin in the way he had intended it? What if she thought he was trying to pay her off or something? What if what if what if—he was driving himself crazy. He had kissed the coin before giving it to

Nick to pass along. Surely she could feel the emotion behind it. Again, he hoped so.

Before closing, Matthew was putting up the bottles and wiping down the tables. Zack had already gone upstairs to bed. Since the shooting, Zack still wasn't back to his whole self. So Matthew had to clean the saloon by himself. He didn't mind. He always appreciated Zack's help, but Matthew was perfectly capable of doing the cleaning by himself. Besides, the mindless work gave him more time to think of Sarah.

The following day was Monday—she had to come to town. She just had to. If she didn't, Matthew didn't know what he was going to do. He had already waited for her much longer than he thought he would have to. And still, he wasn't willing to go to the future to find her and bring her back. It was something he just couldn't do. Something that he wouldn't do. No matter what.

Matthew went to sleep that night with a knowing that he would see Sarah before the next day had passed by. Nick had talked to her Saturday, she would spend Sunday packing, and Monday she would return to Red Bluff —return to him.

When he awoke the next morning, he felt lighter, more buoyant, than before. It was almost as if he could feel Sarah's presence already with him. He quickly dressed and walked out the door and into the hallway. Then he opened the door to Sarah's room. It looked fine. There was nothing he needed to do to make it presentable for Sarah.

He fixed breakfast, which he shared companionably with Zack, neither of them mentioning Sarah. And yet, she was on both of their minds. It seemed funny. Although she hadn't been coming to the saloon that long,

219

she *had* made an impression. A big one. Zack may not be in love with her like he was, but Matthew knew that Zack felt as empty without her as he did. It was like Sarah was larger than life.

Morning passed and afternoon came. Matthew had watched intently every time those swinging doors moved. And finally, suddenly, the swinging doors pushed open and Sarah stood there, expectantly. Matthew put down the bottle he was holding and ran to her. He wrapped his arms around her and wouldn't let go.

"Sarah! Sarah! You came back!"

Zack, who had been in the back kitchen, rushed out and gave her a one-armed hug. "Good to see you, Sarah. So glad you're back!"

"Zack, are you okay?" asked Sarah. She reached out and touched his arm that was in a sling.

"Oh, yeah, I'm fine, Sarah! Just a little gunshot wound, no big deal," he said, acting a little proud that he had gotten it.

Sarah put one hand on both men. "Thank you. Both of you. For rescuing me and for taking care of the outlaws. I appreciate it more than I can say. I love you both." And she embraced both of them.

Two men at the poker table were waving their arms in the air. "I'll leave you two alone now," said Zack. He kissed Sarah on the cheek. "Glad you're back!"

Matthew noticed that Zack winked at him as he walked to the bar to retrieve the whiskey bottle to serve the men. He gently grabbed hold of Sarah's hand.

"Come on, Sarah. Let's sit over here and talk," said Matthew.

CHAPTER FIFTY-SEVEN

SARAH HAD WONDERED how she'd feel when she finally saw him. Were the feelings all in her head? Was it just another fantasy, like it had been with Marcus in the past? But as Matthew led her to a corner table holding her hand, she knew it was real. Her heart felt like it would explode with all the love that she felt for him.

Matthew held out a chair for her, she sat down, and he pulled up a chair next to her. He held her hand and looked into her eyes.

"I love you, Sarah," he said.

"I love you, too, Matthew. I love you so much."

Matthew looked down at their clasped hands and said nothing more. Was he about to propose to her? It felt like that kind of moment, but Matthew stayed silent. Sarah didn't know if she should break the silence or let Matthew have time to build up his courage to ask her. That's what she thought he was doing.

"I missed you so much, Sarah. I was afraid I would never see you again."

Sarah squeezed his hand and said, "You could always have come to the future to see me."

221

Matthew slowly shook his head as he looked at her. "No, I can't do that—wouldn't do that. I'm not that kind of man. Does that bother you?"

Sarah smiled at his expectant look. "No, Matthew. I understand. I guess it's lucky that I love it here so much!" That would surely make him understand that she would stay here, in case that's why he was hesitating, thought Sarah. "Besides, until I found out the outlaws were dealt with, I couldn't return, either."

"I'm so glad you understand, Sarah, so glad."

Matthew looked at her with pleading eyes. What more does he want, Sarah wondered. She was right here, looking at him with love, waiting for him to propose so she could say yes, yes, a thousand times yes! But still, Matthew stayed silent. Sarah didn't think she should interrupt his thoughts.

A thought occurred to Sarah. She remembered Matthew saying that his wife, Catherin, had proposed to him. She thought maybe that Matthew was now waiting for her to propose to him. That's not going to happen, thought Sarah. Whether that was the custom in the old Red Bluff, she didn't know. What she did know was that she was not the kind of woman to ask the man to marry her. It felt like begging. She wasn't going to beg any man to marry her. If he loved her enough, then he would ask her. Period.

A sudden rush of people walked into the saloon interrupting her thoughts. Matthew had to go help Zack, who couldn't handle it all with only one arm. He stood up, leaned over, and kissed Sarah on the forehead. "Love you," he said, as he walked away.

Sarah sat there a minute, smiling, watching him, watching him glance at her and smile. Then she realized that her bags were still on the back of Dancer's saddle. She walked back outside, feeling like her feet didn't reach the floor. It felt so good to be back. It truly did feel like home. She was happy to be home.

When she got to Dancer, she noticed that Josiah and Jenna were getting off their horses in front of the sheriff's office. Sarah waved. Jenna came running over and hugged Sarah. "You're back! Great to see you here again!"

Josiah walked over and hugged Sarah. "Good to see you again, Sarah. Glad you're back." He looked at the two big bags on Dancer. "Would you like me to carry these into the hotel for you?"

"Well, you can carry them, but not into the hotel. I'm staying in a room up here now," said Sarah, motioning to the saloon.

"Oh," said Josiah, raising his eyebrows. "I'll take them up for you."

"You know where Matthew's apartment is? I'm in the room right next to it."

"Ah, okay," said Josiah, as he unhooked the bags from the saddle. Hoisting the two bags onto his shoulders, he pushed through the swinging doors into the saloon.

"Do you have a few minutes, Jenna? Can you come in and talk?" asked Sarah.

"Sure! Let's go," said Jenna.

They walked in and sat at a table by the piano. Zack, one-handed, brought them two glasses of sarsaparilla on a tray.

"Thanks, Zack," both said in unison.

When Zack had walked away, Jenna said, "Sarah, I'm sorry I didn't come back and tell you that it was safe to return here. But I thought that it was Matthew's place to tell you."

"That's okay, Jenna. It worked out. Nick told me. Matthew's not like Josiah. Matthew couldn't come to the future to get me, like Josiah got you. He's not like that. I understand. It doesn't bother me or anything."

"Oh, that's good. Is it good to be back?"

"You don't know how much. You just don't know how good it feels. Hey, I sold my condo!"

"Really? That was fast! How did that happen?"

"Before I came here last time, I had put it up for sale. When I returned after the kidnapping, I wanted to take it off the market, but someone had already bought it! Then he wanted to move in after thirty days. So he paid me twenty thousand more than my asking price for it— just to take possession in thirty days!"

"Wow. That's awesome!"

"And I quit my job!"

"You're kidding!"

"Marcus asked me once too often to pick up his dry cleaning. I quit and just walked out!"

"Wow, Sarah, I can't believe you did that. He probably won't give you a good recommendation now."

Sarah shook her head. "I don't need it. I'm here now. I have a job," and she nodded toward the piano.

Jenna smiled. "Then you almost have it all." She nodded toward Matthew.

"Almost is right. He said he loves me, but he didn't ask me to marry him. I think he wants me to ask him!"

"So ask!"

"No, I'm not going to do that. Do they do it that way here? You know, in the nineteenth century?"

"No. Josiah asked me. I think it's the same here as in the future. The man usually asks, but there is nothing

224

stopping a woman from asking. Just go for it, Sarah. You two love each other. Just ask *him*!"

Sarah shook her head again. "No, I'm not going to do it. I'll just wait him out!"

Jenna laughed. "Whatever."

"Oh, Jenna, you wouldn't believe what else! Remember you told me that Marcus and his wife were happily married? Guess what? They're getting a divorce!"

"No!" said Jenna, shocked.

Sarah started telling Jenna about Marcus coming to her condo and everything he said to her. Then Josiah approached the table.

"You ready, Jenna?"

"Give me a few more minutes, Josiah. I have to hear this."

After Josiah sat down at the bar to wait, Sarah continued the story. She told Jenna about how Marcus had returned the following day and had even tried the door handle.

"I can't believe it," said Jenna. "I just can't believe it. What did you do, then?"

"That's when I moved into your place with Madison." She stopped suddenly and looked at Jenna. "That's all right, isn't it?"

"Sure, Sarah, of course. But you're here now, anyway, so it doesn't matter."

Just then, a regular called out, "Sarah! Play the piano for us!" Then the rest of the people in the bar started chanting, "Sarah! Sarah!"

She smiled, nodded to Jenna, and took a couple of steps to the piano. Jenna left the table and stood next to Josiah at the bar. When Sarah started singing, Jenna looked back at her and smiled. Sarah, since that first day when Josiah hadn't recognized the song that she sang, had been careful to sing only those songs that were available in the nineteenth century. But today, she belted out, "Wind Beneath My Wings." And as she sang it, she looked at Matthew the whole time.

CHAPTER FIFTY-EIGHT

SARAH WAS SO happy to be back in the old Red Bluff singing again that the hours flew by. She couldn't believe that it was already time to close the saloon. Matthew had a habit of putting everything away before it was time to close. She had watched him do this again and again in the past weeks. So when he finally closed the doors, he was finished and could go upstairs.

Sarah watched as he pulled the main door closed on the swinging doors. She had always wondered about that when she watched old westerns. Didn't they ever close the saloon? Since she had been here, she had taken it for granted. There was an interior regular door, *inside* the swinging doors. It was that interior door that remained closed when they weren't open.

Matthew walked over to her as she finished singing her song. He picked up her tip glass and looked. "I know!" said Sarah. "It's the most tips I've ever received in one night!"

"They missed you," said Matthew.

Then he smiled and took her hand. This was her first night sleeping upstairs above the saloon. She didn't know why, but she felt nervous about it. Then she remembered the composting toilet and was happy again. And now she even had regular toilet paper! Life was good.

She and Matthew walked up the stairs hand in hand. Matthew stopped in front of Sarah's door and hugged her.

"I'm so glad you're home, Sarah. So glad."

"I'm glad to be home, Matthew. I love you." Then she kissed him gently on the lips.

"Good night, Sarah, see you in the morning."

Sarah looked at him as he tried to walk away. But she had taken his hand and intertwined their fingers.

"Matthew, I would feel much safer if you were with me."

Matthew shook his head and said, "Oh, Sarah, I—"

"Please, Matthew. I want to feel safe." Then she opened the door and encouraged him to walk inside with her.

The following morning, Sarah woke up late. Matthew had already left her room. She rummaged around until she found her smartphone so she could look at the time. 9:30. Oh! She had to hurry. Before Jenna left the night before, they had arranged to meet for a late breakfast at the hotel restaurant across the street.

After getting dressed and ready, Sarah walked downstairs. Matthew had already opened the saloon. A few people were at the poker table, but no one she recognized. She walked up to Matthew, behind the bar, and kissed him on the lips.

"Good morning, beautiful," he said.

"Good morning, handsome. I'm going to have breakfast with Jenna. I'll be back soon."

"I love you."

"Love you, too, Matthew."

Sarah walked across the street feeling like she had it all. He hadn't asked her to marry him yet, but she felt sure that would come in time. She could wait. The most important thing is that she was home now, and Matthew loved her.

She walked into the hotel. When Eliza saw her, she said, "Congratulations, Sarah!"

"Congratulations, Sarah!" said Samuel, Eliza's husband.

Granny and Edward were walking down the stairs. "Hey, Sarah, congratulations. Now you can be as miserable as the rest of us," Granny joked.

"Not half as miserable as you're goin' to be after I beat you," said Edward, as he hugged Granny with one hand and pretended to hit her with the other.

Sarah, confused, walked into the restaurant. She was happy to see Jenna there.

When she sat down, Jenna said, "I'd say congratulations, Sarah, but you look confused."

"Why is everybody congratulating me?"

Jenna shook her head. "Ah-oh. I thought it might be something like this when I saw your face."

"What?"

"Matthew has told everyone that you and he are getting married."

"What! He never asked me!"

"Apparently he must think that you asked him!"

"I never asked him! I—wait—do you think—?"

"What? Tell me," said Jenna.

Sarah leaned over the table and whispered to Jenna, "We slept together last night."

"That's it, Sarah. As far as he's concerned, that was

your proposal. He's already arranged for the minister to come this weekend."

"You're kidding! That little—"

"Easy, girl. These are Victorian times." Jenna laughed. "Matthew took that as a proposal. You can't blame him. These are different times."

Eliza brought their breakfast in. Eggs and coffee. "So good to have you back, Sarah. Matthew is a good man. You two will be happy together."

Sarah was about to say something to clarify the situation when Jenna nudged her under the table. "Thank you, Eliza," she said instead. When Eliza walked away, Sarah said, "What did you do that for?"

"This is between you and Matthew. You don't need to involve anyone else. What difference does it make anyway? You want to marry him, don't you? You love him, right?"

"Yes, I love him, and I do want to marry him. I thought he'd ask me yesterday, and it surprised me when he didn't. But like this?"

"Let it go, Sarah. You want to marry him, just marry him. Who cares if he thinks you proposed or not? You both want the same thing."

"I don't know. It annoys me." She stood up. "I'm going to talk to him right now." Sarah wiped her mouth, then stomped out of the restaurant and across the street to the saloon.

CHAPTER FIFTY-NINE

MATTHEW FELT ELATED. He was marrying the woman he loved, and he couldn't be happier about it. She had asked him last night. Well, she didn't ask him in words, but it amounted to the same thing, right? He could read the signs as well as any man, and that sign said, "Let's get married!" And that was exactly what he wanted.

He had tried to get her to ask him when they sat at the table the previous day. As he stared intently into her eyes, he had tried to send her the thought to ask him to get married. But she hadn't understood him—or she did, but didn't want to ask him with words. That was all right. It all ended up the same. They would marry and be together for all time. That was good enough for him.

When Sarah came through the door with such an angry look on her face, Matthew didn't understand. She didn't even look at him. Walking straight to Zack, she whispered something to him, and he stood up immediately and walked behind the bar.

Sarah, with narrowed eyes, said, "We need to talk, Matthew."

"Okay," he said.

231

"*Not* here."

"Let's go in the back," said Matthew.

"Upstairs, now!"

"Oh, okay."

Sarah led the way upstairs, stomping on each stair as she went. She walked past her own door, and continued to his. Then she opened it, walked in, and sat down at the table. Matthew followed.

"You told everyone we were getting married!"

"We are!" said Matthew.

"I don't recall you asking me to marry you."

"I didn't! You asked me!"

"What!" It wasn't a question.

"You asked me! Well, maybe not in words, but—" Matthew smiled and motioned with his head toward her room.

"No! That was not a proposal for marriage! That is not how it works in my time."

"Yeah, but I thought—"

"You thought wrong, Matthew! I'm not marrying you!"

"Why not? I thought you loved me."

"I do love you, but that's not enough."

"What do you mean, not enough?"

Matthew suddenly saw a gleam in Sarah's eyes. It scared him. The whole conversation scared him.

"Okay, Matthew. If you won't ask me to marry you, but you want to marry me, I'll make you a deal."

"Fine. What's the deal?"

"Come to the future with me."

"Oh, no."

"Not permanently. Just to see it, experience it. Find out where I come from."

232

"Knowing where you come from is good enough for me. I can't go there. I told you—I'm not that kind of man. I want to stay in Red Bluff and never leave."

Matthew could see that Sarah was fuming. She slammed her fist onto the table.

"You're impossible! How did Catherin get you to move out west?"

He shrugged his shoulders. "She threatened to leave me." As soon as he said it, he knew it was a mistake. Although he didn't have a choice, because he wouldn't lie to her.

Sarah smiled, didn't say a word, and stood up. He looked up at her questioningly. She walked to the door, opened it, and stood in the doorway.

"Matthew, unless you come to the future with me—to visit—we're finished."

Matthew smiled. Surely she was joking. He shook his head. "Sorry, Sarah, I can't do that."

"Are you prepared to lose me, then?"

"What do you mean?"

"I mean, it's not just that I won't marry you, if you don't go with me. I mean that I'm leaving here and never returning. No more piano, no more singing, no more Sarah in the nineteenth century. I'm done." She started to close the door and opened it enough to stick her head back in. "I mean it, Matthew, so you better think about it before you give me an answer." Then she closed the door —hard, and walked down the hallway.

Matthew sat at the table and put his head in his hands. He couldn't go to the future. He just couldn't. On the other hand, he also couldn't lose Sarah. There was no way he could let that happen.

The whole situation made him angry with Catherin.

If she hadn't forced him to come west, then he wouldn't have had to tell Sarah why he came here. But if Catherin hadn't forced him, then he never would have met Sarah. Dang. What could he do?

Matthew sat there a long time weighing the possibilities. In the end, he knew there was just one. He had to go with Sarah to the future. If that's what it took for her to stay here and marry him, then he would do it. Once. For her.

He walked downstairs and looked around in the saloon, but he didn't see her. Then he told Zack he could take it from there.

"Is everything all right with Sarah?" asked Zack.

"It is now," said Matthew.

"Are you still getting married?"

"I hope so."

CHAPTER SIXTY

MATTHEW WAS BEHIND the bar washing glasses when Sarah walked in. The movement of the swinging doors caught his attention. She wasn't smiling. There was a funny look on her face—like she was afraid. His fists unconsciously balled up as he wondered who had made her afraid. Then he relaxed as it dawned on him: she was afraid that he would say no. He felt bad that he had made his beautiful Sarah afraid. Because he didn't want her to be afraid of anything ever again.

She walked up to him at the bar, but didn't say anything, just looked into his eyes. As he looked at her, he said, "Zack," and Zack came behind the bar. Matthew walked out and took Sarah's hand. "Let's talk," he said.

They walked up the stairs in silence, holding hands. He opened the door for her and followed her inside his apartment. They sat at the table like before.

Still holding her hand, Matthew looked into her eyes and smiled. "Yes, Sarah, I'll go with you. I can't lose you now."

Sarah looked down, and he saw tears drop from her eyes onto her lap. "I was afraid you would say no."

"I hate that you're making me do this, but there is no way I could lose you now."

She held up Matthew's hand that she had been holding and kissed it. "I love you, Matthew. We can go this weekend. I already talked to Jenna, and she'll watch the bar for you when we go."

"We can't go on the weekend, Sarah. That's when the minister is coming."

Sarah pulled her hand away and narrowed her eyes. "If you think you can trick me into marrying you and then not go to the future with me, you've got another think coming, mister!"

He patted her hand. "No, Sarah. I thought we'd go tomorrow. The sooner we get this over with the better. Is tomorrow okay?"

"I'd rather go on the weekend, because then I could get Madison to come here or something, so we could be alone in the house overnight."

"No, not overnight. You didn't say anything about overnight."

"Matthew, it's one night. If you're going all the way there, we might as well stay one measly night."

"All the way there? I thought it was only an hour away."

"An hour, yes, but it is more than a hundred years away."

"Oh. I'm still not happy with overnight."

"I have a lot to show you. Please stay just one night."

Matthew, resigned, shook his head. "All right. One night, but no more. And this weekend, we get married."

"All right. I'll marry you—even if you didn't ask me." Matthew smiled shyly at her, and she continued. "Maybe, instead of Jenna, I could get Eliza to watch the saloon, and we could double date with Jenna and Josiah!"

"No. I'll do this, but just with you. No one else around. Just you and me."

"Okay, okay. Just you and me. I'm fine with that."

"What's a double date?" Matthew asked.

"When two couples go on an outing together. One couple going out is called a date. So two couples is a double date."

"Okay. Just me and you. No double date. And we go tomorrow."

Sarah leaned over and kissed him. "I love you, Matthew."

"I love you, too, Sarah."

CHAPTER SIXTY-ONE

AFTER A BRIEF delay for breakfast, picking up Dancer and a second horse, they were on their way. Matthew had insisted that he could not face the future on an empty stomach, regardless of what a "coffee shop" was. But finally, here they were on the trail that led to the cave.

When they reached the entrance to the cave, Sarah stopped Dancer. "Are you ready for this, my love?" she asked Matthew.

"No," said Matthew.

"But you're going, right?"

"Let's do it before I change my mind."

Without another word, Sarah let Dancer enter the cave. Matthew's horse followed. Halfway through, Matthew said, "Are we in the future yet?"

"Everyone asks that. But I have no idea where the past ends and the future begins. We're almost to the other side of the cave, though."

When they rode out into the bright sunshine, Matthew said, "Is this the future, then?"

"Yes, we are now in the new Red Bluff."

"Okay, I did it. I came to the future like you asked and

now I want to go back."

Matthew started to turn his horse around, but Sarah was too quick. She grabbed his reins and proceeded down the trail. Matthew had no choice but to follow.

"Stop gritting your teeth. We'll be there soon."

"How did you know I was gritting my teeth?"

Sarah laughed. "Just a lucky guess."

A short time later, Sarah was off Dancer opening the gate to Jenna's pasture. Matthew rode in. Sarah closed the gate and climbed back onto Dancer's back. After a few more minutes, they were at the paddock. They got off their horses, and Sarah led them into the barn. Sarah unsaddled both horses and put the saddles away. Then she got brushes and handed one to Matthew.

"Brush your horse," she said.

"I haven't brushed a horse in years," said Matthew.

"Don't worry. It will come back to you. It's like riding a bicycle."

"What's a bicycle?" asked Matthew.

Sarah chuckled and shook her head. "Never mind. Just brush."

Fifteen minutes later, brushes put away, they walked toward the ranch house. Then Matthew noticed the cars. There were several. So many people had moved to the old Red Bluff, and they had all left their cars here: Jenna of course, Granny, Ryan, Sarah's car was there, and Rachel, who was in Red Bluff most of the time now, had also left her car there. Matthew looked in a car window and ran his hand along the outside.

"Wow," said Matthew. "So this is a car. Where's a truck?"

Sarah pointed to the two-car garage. "See over there? That's Jenna's pickup truck. They get much bigger than that, though." Then Sarah led him into the house.

When they entered the living room, Sarah took the remote control off the television and stepped back. "Check it out," she said and clicked the remote on.

When the weather channel came on the screen, Matthew stepped back in amazement. "What *is* that thing?"

"It's called a television. Everyone has one. Look at this." Sarah clicked through all the channels, which thrilled Matthew. "Come on, there's more," said Sarah, as she turned off the set and led him into the kitchen.

"Since you do a lot of cooking, you'll appreciate what's in the kitchen." She opened the refrigerator. "This keeps food cold all the time. Stick your hand in and feel this," she pointed to the milk.

"Oh! It's cold! Wow!"

Sarah opened the freezer section and asked him to stick his hand in again. Matthew reached inside and touched the box of ice cream. "That's *really* cold!"

"Frozen. The top part of the refrigerator is called a freezer, because it freezes everything." She walked over to the dishwasher and opened it. "You put dirty dishes in here, turn it on, and it washes them for you." Then she walked to the glass top electric stove. "This is how we cook our food." She opened the front of the oven.

"That's where you put the wood?"

"No wood, Matthew. Nobody cooks with wood any-more. This stove cooks with electricity, which I'll explain later." She closed the oven door and walked to the microwave. "This is called a microwave oven. It heats food and liquids really fast. Open that cabinet and give me a cup."

Matthew picked up a cup and handed it to her. Sarah

took the cup, brought it to the sink, and turned on the water. "I forgot the water. Did you see this?"

Matthew smiled and shook his head. Sarah walked back to the microwave, opened the door, and then turned to Matthew. "Here, stick your finger in here." She held up the cupful of cold water for him.

"It's cold. So what?"

Sarah tossed her head. "So what, he asks. Just you wait." She put the cup into the microwave and set the timer for a minute. When it rang she took it out and held it out for Matthew. "Stick your finger in, but be careful."

Matthew stuck his finger in. "Ouch! It's hot!"

"Fast, isn't it? Now let's go into the bathroom." Sarah led him to the main bathroom. "Come on in, don't be afraid. You know that toilet that you got me? This is one, a little different—well, a lot different—that everyone in the new Red Bluff has." She demonstrated how the toilet flushed.

"Everyone has one of these?"

"Yes, everyone. This house has three of them."

"Three? Why would you need three?"

"When there's several people in the house, there's no waiting."

"How often do you have to move it?" Matthew asked.

"It's not like an outhouse, Matthew." She explained to him the basics on how a sewer worked. He was fascinated. They walked toward the front, and Sarah stopped at the thermostat. "This controls the heat in the house. You set the temperature that makes you feel comfortable, and the heater keeps it at that temperature." She walked him down the hall to a heating vent. "The heat comes out of here."

"No fire for this, either?"

Sarah shook her head. "No fire."

"Wow."

"Come on, I want to take you to town now. We'll take my car."

Matthew's eyes got big. "Are you sure?"

"Sure. It won't hurt. You'll think it's fun. Come on."

A few minutes later, they were driving down the street with Matthew's seat belt pulled extra tight, so he could barely breathe. He had one white-knuckled hand on the armrest and one white-knuckled hand on the dashboard.

"Don't worry" said Sarah. "I'm a good driver.

"Let's see, where should we go? It's too early for lunch. Oh, I know!" Sarah pulled over to the curb. "I pulled over so you could feel safe. Do you have any gold coins in your pocket?"

"You want one now? Why?"

"You'll see. Just check."

Matthew reached into his pocket and pulled out two of them. "Two."

"Good. Hold onto them. I know where we'll go." Sarah drove to the coin store and parked in front. "Let's go in."

They walked in, and Matthew found all the different coins on display interesting. Then Sarah told him to give the man one gold coin.

"What do you want for it this time, Sarah?"

"The usual. Silver dollars, halves, quarters, whatever you have." Several minutes later, the man was counting out fifteen hundred dollars worth of coins. When Matthew started to protest, she subtly motioned him to stop. He scooped up the coins and put them in his pocket. Back in the car, Matthew said, "Explain, please."

"Gold coins are worth a lot more here."

"Yes, but all this?"

"Gold is worth a lot of money in this century. The silver dollars are worth about fifteen dollars each—depending on the year, but gold is worth a ton more. Are you getting hungry yet?"

"Starved. Coming to the future is hard work!" Matthew rubbed his stomach, and they both laughed.

"Where should we go for lunch? There are so many places to choose from here."

"The tiger restaurant."

"Tiger? What's that?"

"Josiah told me about it. He said that he and Jenna go to the tiger restaurant."

"Tiger, tiger, tiger? I don't know any tiger—oh! I bet you mean the Thai restaurant!"

"Yes! That's what Jenna called it. Thai!"

When they walked in, Matthew looked around in wonder. He saw strange pictures on the walls of unfamiliar stone figures, elephants, and people dressed in strange ways. There were statues of elephants all around, also. Sarah enjoyed watching his face as he looked around.

When they sat down, Sarah said, "Would you mind if I order for you? Do you like chicken?"

"Go ahead. You know what's good. Yes, chicken is good."

While they waited for their food, Sarah watched as Matthew kept looking around. Every once in a while, he would look back at her and smile. Finally, he said, "This place, your world, is nothing like I expected. I don't know exactly what I expected, but it wasn't this."

"Do you mind it?"

"No, but don't get any ideas. I don't want to live here."

Sarah laughed. "I don't, either. I want to live in the

243

old Red Bluff, with you."

Then their meal came. It was Sarah's favorite dish at this restaurant. A pineapple carved out, with chicken, pineapple, miniature corn, and some other vegetables, all stir fried and put back into the pineapple. It was delicious.

Matthew started eating slowly, not knowing what to think. Then he looked at her and said, "Delicious! Sarah, this is fantastic! I wonder if I could make this."

"I'd love to have you try. It's my favorite dish in the world."

For dessert, they ordered fried bananas and sticky rice with Thai coconut custard. They shared them, and Matthew couldn't stop smiling.

"You like this, don't you?" asked Sarah.

"Yes, but I still don't want to live here!"

When they finished and waited for the bill, Matthew just stared at Sarah. She looked back at him and smiled. Then he reached over, took her hand, and said, "Sarah James, will you marry me?"

She grabbed his face and kissed it, while tears slid down her face. "Of course I'll marry you! I told you I would!"

"You did, but I didn't officially ask you. Now, I have."

"Thank you, Matthew. That means a lot to me."

"It took me awhile, but I finally realized that."

Although Matthew wanted to pay the bill because of all the money he had in his pocket, Sarah convinced him not to. It wasn't worth using the expensive coins in the new Red Bluff.

After lunch, they walked down to the ice cream store on the corner. Matthew couldn't believe how many flavors there were to choose from. First he had to sample several, and then he got a triple scoop cone. When he finished, he wanted another one with different flavors. Sarah paid for it and laughed as she watched him eat it.

"Sarah, maybe I was wrong. Maybe I *could* live here!"

"Oh no you don't! *I* don't want to! We'll figure out a way to make flavored ice cream back home!"

When they finally left the ice cream store, Matthew was holding his stomach. Sarah shook her head and drove back to the ranch. Madison's car was there when they arrived.

They walked in, and Madison met them at the door. "Hi, Sarah! Hi, Matthew! Good to see you both!" She noticed Matthew still holding his stomach. "Don't tell me —ice cream and cake!"

"Just ice cream—two triple scoops."

Madison laughed and opened the door for them. "You guys going to spend the night here?"

"Yeah, we were," said Sarah.

"Oh, good, would you mind checking on the horses, then? I was going to stay over at a friend's tonight."

"Of course we can check on the horses, Madison. No problem." She looked at Madison and winked, knowing that she was staying out of the house deliberately. "And thank you!"

Madison smiled and walked to her room at the back of the house. A few minutes later, she came out with a packed bag. "Enjoy yourselves! See you a hundred years ago!"

All three of them laughed, and Matthew sat on the couch in a heap. Sarah sat next to him. "I'm going to go take care of the horses now," said Sarah. "Be back in a minute. Or maybe you should walk around so you don't get sick."

"I just want to sit here. I don't think I can get up again."

Sarah pulled him up. "Come on. Walk around. It will help you digest."

Together, they walked slowly out to the barn. Matthew walked around while Sarah checked to make sure all the horses had food and water. Dancer nickered as she walked by, and she stroked his soft nose. Then she stepped through the gate and found Matthew walking in the pasture.

"I'm feeling better now," he said.

"Do you want to watch a movie?"

"What's a movie?"

They walked into the house and sat down in front of the television. Sarah looked through the TV guide, read the choices to Matthew, and let him decide. They spent the rest of the evening watching movies, eating microwave popcorn, talking, and laughing. When it got late, they went to bed.

It was late morning before they headed back toward the old Red Bluff. They had gone to the store to get a soft ice chest, some ice, two pineapples, and some ice cream. As they rode side by side on their way to the cave, they held hands.

After talking and laughing over all the different experiences that Matthew had while in the new Red Bluff, they turned single file up the steep trail toward the cave. When they emerged on the other side and approached the Red Bluff sign, Matthew took Sarah's hand again.

"You know, Sarah," he said, squeezing her hand, "maybe we *can* double date with Jenna and Josiah. You know, to the Thai restaurant!"

If you liked this book, sign up on our mailing list to be notified of the next Cowgirls in Time book!
www.RalstonStorePublishing.com/cowgirls.html
>>>>>>>>>>>>>>>>>>>>>>>>>>>>>>>>>>>>

AGAINST
THE *Wind*
Cowgirls in Time
Romance

ERICA EINHORN

In *Against the Wind*, read how Madison and Zack fall in love and plan their future, until they realize it is that future that could keep them apart.

Erica Einhorn